M

SILBERMANN

SILBERMANN

Jacques de Lacretelle

FOREWORD BY

Victor Brombert

TRANSLATED FROM THE FRENCH BY

Helen Marx

HELEN MARX BOOKS : NEW YORK

First published in 1922 by Éditions Gallimard.

Copyright © 2004 by Helen Marx Books,
an imprint of Turtle Point Press

LCCN 2001 132724
ISBN 188-55-86-56-6

Edited by Ruth Greenstein

CONTENTS

FOREWORD

Silbermann appeared in 1922, barely four years after the end of the First World War. It is a beautiful but painful book. Behind its apparent simplicity and closely knit structure is a multi-layered novel centered on the persecution of a Jewish student in a Paris lycée. Silbermann, an unusually sensitive, ambitious, intellectually mature adolescent, courageous yet vulnerable, is ultimately forced to leave school and to expatriate himself. But this story is more than the account of a persecution. For Silbermann is not presented directly; he is seen through the eyes of a fellow student who befriends him, and who out of fervent idealism has taken it upon himself to become the champion and defender of the persecuted Jewish boy. Silbermann is therefore not the only subject of this story. The narrator-friend, in the process of describing the events, turns out in a sense to be the central character, revealing his anxieties, his weaknesses, and his own prejudices.

There is still more to this novel: it is about the difficult ties of adolescent friendship in the midst of the cruelty of a group, the tensions between children and their parents, and the themes of sincerity, bad faith, and self-deceit. *Silbermann* also evokes recent social and political history: the chauvinism and xenophobia that followed the Dreyfus case, along with a surge of democratically inspired anti-clerical feelings that led to legislation directed by the Third Republic against the Catholic Church. And with all that, we are also given insights into the mentality of French Protestants who, for centuries a persecuted minority, had been taught to sympathize

FOREWORD

with all victims of persecution. A complex novel indeed.

Jacques de Lacretelle (1888–1985) came from a family with a liberal tradition, with links to anti-clerical milieux that had been sympathetic to the cause of Dreyfus. His mother was Protestant by birth, but neither parent was religious, and Lacretelle did not have a religious upbringing. He attended the Lycée Janson de Sailly, in the upper-class sixteenth arrondissement of Paris. This is the very same lycée that, quite recognizably, is the one described in *Silbermann*, though by Lacretelle's own admission he never witnessed the kind of anti-Jewish hatred he described in his novel.

Silbermann therefore has more than anecdotal value. It raises broader issues related to chauvinism, racism, and persecution. The very word *juif*, for Jew, has an ugly resonance; it is spat out at Silbermann with a contemptuous pout. In such a hostile milieu, where scholastic success only

FOREWORD

exacerbates resentment, the adolescent's inner fire and intellectual energy are soon subdued, leaving him aware of a sense of difference, incurable sadness, and the atavism of deep suffering. It is revealing that this almost abnormally gifted, precocious young Jew is seen by the narrator in terms of moral and physiological stereotypes that deprive him of true individuality. Silbermann displays a mixture of pride, weakness, subservience, arrogance, fear, and the desire to dominate. His specific ugliness is described in caricature-like fashion: his pointed chin, his prominent cheekbones, his hooked nose, his fleshy and pendulous lips, his frizzy hair. These details are revealing because they are repeatedly stressed by the narrator-friend, a witness who can hardly be called objective, since he seems truly obsessed with what he considers his "mission" of self-sacrifice, his yearning to be a martyr in a noble cause, eager to reach the highest summits of ethical behavior, and thus far more pre-

FOREWORD

occupied with himself than with his friend. When his aims and ideals collapse around him, he turns against his friend whom he previously claimed to admire for his mental prowess, now blaming him for his intellectual contradictions, his constant criticisms, his barren recycling of other people's ideas, his poisoning of all pleasure —in other words, for being a destructive Jew.

The rejection of former enthusiasms and alliances is a central theme in this novel. The narrator rebels against his parents whom he previously revered. He grew up proud of his family's Protestant sense of duty, moral standards, and work ethics. When his parents' underlying hypocrisy is revealed to him, his own values collapse.

In developing this theme of adolescent disillusionment and rebellion, Lacretelle follows a trend set by other writers well into the 1920s. André Gide (1869–1951) had a significant impact on the author of *Silbermann*. Even the titles

FOREWORD

of some of Gide's best known works—*The Return of the Prodigal Son* (1907), *Strait is the Gate* (1909), *The Pastoral Symphony* (1919)—are relevant to a better understanding of Lacretelle's novel. Among Gide's favorite subjects are the many ways in which moral purpose, as well as the quest for sincerity and authenticity, can thrive on duplicity and bad faith.

Not just literary fashions but political events are reflected in *Silbermann*. The Dreyfus case, which exploded in 1894, ended with the unjustly condemned Jewish captain being belatedly vindicated thanks to the courageous intervention of Émile Zola, Anatole France, large numbers of intellectuals, and many others who were scandalized by the deliberate miscarriage of justice resulting from the military establishment's falsification and concealment of the truth. The infamous affair divided and embittered French society, explaining on one hand the almost fanatical anti-clerical, anti-Catholic legislation known as the Combes Law of 1905,

FOREWORD

which expelled religious congregations, and, on the other, an exacerbation of chauvinism and anti-Semitism.

Silbermann must thus be read as a multiple indictment. It is a radical denunciation of Jew-hatred, viewed as irrational, violent, and profoundly dishonest. The anti-Semite sets up the Jew in his otherness. One could even say that he existentially creates the Jew as the other-to-be-hated.

But the novel, articulated through the narrator's voice, is also an indictment of the narrator's own latent anti-Jewish prejudices. For excessive admiration of Jewish abilities and Jewish intelligence can also betray a form of racism—the anti-Semitism of the well-intentioned.

Ultimately, *Silbermann* tells us something about Lacretelle's own hesitation between conflicting views of the Jew as the eternal foreigner and the Jew as a creation of those who feel the need to hate. In the process, he has written the story of a multiple defeat. The end of the novel

FOREWORD

could not be more bitter. Silbermann has been driven away from school and forced to emigrate to America, where he will become a diamond dealer instead of the French writer he hoped to be. And his former friend now agrees with one of the persecutors that the coarse charcoal caricature of the ungainly young Jew still visible on a wall is indeed a very good likeness. Beneath the caricature the words "Death to the Jews" are still legible.

Lacretelle shows himself to be a subtle analyst of the human soul, in the best tradition of the French *roman d'analyse*. But the message of the book is one of disquieting pessimism. There seems to be no way of escaping one's self and one's tragic destiny.

VICTOR BROMBERT

Henry Putnam Professor of Comparative and Romance Literature Emeritus, Princeton University

SILBERMANN

CHAPTER

1

Entering the tenth grade meant attending the upper school. It occupied one half of the building and was identical to the other half, where I had spent the last four years: the same courtyard with a few trees in it, surrounded by a high covered gallery that opened out in one place to form a playground; the same layout of classrooms along the gallery; and on the walls between the windows, similar casts of antique bas-reliefs.

Nevertheless, since that October morning was my first time in that particular courtyard, everything seemed new, and I looked all around with great curiosity. The freshly painted doors and windowsills made me vaguely regret the end of my independence. Their reddish-brown color was like that of the berries I had picked only the day before in the garden at Aiguesbelles, our farmhouse near Nîmes. We had spent our vacation there with my grandparents, just as we did every year, and had stayed until the evening of the last Sunday. My mother loved those days of ritual and laziness, which reminded her of her childhood. My father's absence—he had returned to Paris at the beginning of September—left her free to spend the days as she once had. In the morning we went to church with my grandparents. On the way back my mother never failed to pick the finest and warmest fig from the old fig tree, whose gnarled roots were entwined around the terrace flagstones. She would hand it to me, having cut the rosy, grainy flesh into four pieces, and watch me eat it to see if I enjoyed it as much as she had at my age ...

Despite my feelings of apprehension over the renewed constraints of school, I was happily impatient as I stood in the courtyard waiting to see my friend Philippe Robin. He wasn't there yet because the pupils at the Catholic institution where he was a part-time boarder arrived at the lycée just in time for class. While waiting for him in the midst of the general commotion, I had shaken a few hands and exchanged a few greetings in a reserved, noncommittal way, carefully saving any real emotion for Philippe. In any case, I didn't really know most of the students around me, only the stories I'd made up about them from seeing them come and go in the past.

The group from St. Xavier's finally appeared. At the head were *de* Montclar and *de* La Béchellière (our teachers always used the prefix). Both of them had been in the ninth grade with me. Montclar was medium-sized and sturdy with strong features and had assumed the arrogant air he always put on when coming to school. He cast contemptuous glances left and right and made sneering remarks to his companion. La Béchellière was tall, had a long neck, and looked arrogant, too, but he was narrow-chested and undeveloped, and his mincing manner was affected. When one asked him a question, his only response was the silly expression on his pasty face. At last I caught sight of Philippe running toward me.

How he had changed! I couldn't help exclaiming when I saw him up close. His skin was tanned and there was yellow fuzz on his cheeks; when he laughed his dimples deepened, leaving little wrinkles.

"Well!" he said proudly. "I've gotten a marvelous sunburn. As I wrote you, I was at Arcachon, where I spent the month of September with my Uncle Marc. We either fished or shot seabirds all day long. Sometimes we'd leave at four in the morning and come back that night ... And it wasn't easy, my friend, shooting curlews. There's no bird more cunning or more difficult to shoot. My uncle said so. He killed only four during the season, although he always wins prizes in clay-pigeon contests."

I had never held a gun. Hunting held ab-

4

solutely no appeal for me. I knew Philippe's uncle slightly. He was about thirty years old, athletic looking, with a big red moustache and an iron handshake.

Philippe broke off and absentmindedly asked me, "And you? Did you come back yesterday? . . . Did you have a good vacation?"

"Oh, I love Aiguesbelles!" I said. "Every year I like it more."

"Well, me too. I've never had as much fun as in these last two months, especially at Arcachon."

He resumed his stories. He told me about an incident in which a boat had overturned and about the sailing regattas in which he had taken part. He talked on and on in a bragging tone of voice, paying no attention whatsoever to me. I remembered the enormous disappointment I had felt as a child one day when a friend I had gone to see played all by himself, throwing a ball very high up in the air and then catching it. Philippe rattled on, his face flushed with pleasure, about this crazy, happy life in which I played no part, where everything was foreign to me. That flush of excitement was so unpleasant and seemed like such positive proof of his deep disloyalty to me that I turned my head away. As I gazed down at the dusty gravel of the courtyard, I sadly remembered how for weeks I had looked forward with pleasure to our reunion . . . I had a premonition that we were no longer going to be friends.

The drum rolled. We lined up.

"At Houlgate, during the month of August," he continued in a lower tone of voice, "I played a lot of tennis. But it was less agreeable because" —and at this point he made a face—"there were too many Jews . . . On the beach, at the casino, everywhere, that's all you ran into. Uncle Marc didn't even want to stay for three days. Hey, that boy was there. His name's Silbermann."

As he said this, he pointed out a boy standing in the front row by the classroom door, whom I hadn't remembered seeing the year before in any division of ninth grade. He was short and very slight. His face, which I could see clearly because he was turning around and talking to his neighbors, was very mature but fairly ugly, with prominent cheekbones and a pointed chin. His complexion was pale and yellowish, his eyes and eyebrows were dark, and his lips were fleshy and pink. He had highly animated gestures, which attracted one's attention. One couldn't help watching his mimicry, which was for the benefit of those nearest him, as his pupils darted from one person to another. The whole scene seemed bizarrely precocious; he reminded me of those infant prodigies performing their acts in a circus. I found it hard to stop staring.

We entered the classroom. The St. Xavier boys, about ten of them, formed their own group, as usual; I sat in front of Philippe Robin. As soon as Silbermann came in, he raced to the foot of the teacher's desk with a triumphant air. Our professor was around forty with a cold, piercing look and very precise movements. He proceeded to ask each of us a series of questions, taking notes as we answered. We learned that Silbermann had skipped a grade. This was a fairly rare occurrence and required some explanation.

"I was a whole year behind," he said, "and have to make it up. I did very well in ninth grade."

"I don't think you'll be able to keep up."

"I won three prizes last year," he insisted.

"That's all very well, but you're not as well prepared in our subjects as your classmates are. The school curriculum is carefully graduated, and anybody who misses a rung in the ladder risks falling."

"I worked during the vacation, Sir."

During this dialogue Silbermann remained standing and spoke in a humble tone of voice. But in spite of this exemplary stance and attitude, his desire to persuade the teacher made his voice echo weirdly in the classroom. As we were being let out for break, someone came up to him, shrugging his shoulders: "Look, you can't stay in this class. You must go back to the ninth grade."

"Do you think so?" answered Silbermann sarcastically. Then, with an emphatic gesture of his hand and a slight sneer: "How much do you want to bet that I'll be first, at least twice, before the end of the term?"

We were given the afternoon off that first day, and Philippe Robin came by to see me. My family found him charming. My father held up his assured manner and my mother his politeness as examples for me. They had very much encouraged our friendship. The first time I mentioned his name in front of my mother, she asked if he lived on the Avenue Hoche, and when I answered affirmatively, she had said approvingly, "Then he's the son of the lawyer. They're a very well-known family and a big name in the Paris bourgeoisie. The Robins have been practicing law for about a hundred years."

DE LACRETELLE : SILBERMANN

It was she who suggested I ask him over. I know very well why. Since her marriage, my mother's only interest in life had been her husband's career. With single-minded determination and patience she had pursued anything that could advance or bolster my father's career. She was most certainly not about to relax her efforts now since, as she said, my father, as an examining magistrate in Paris, was only halfway there. But I was approaching adulthood, and like a faithful old horse who only knows how to perform one thing, she was prepared to do the same for me. She often spoke about my future, explaining various professions, their advantages and disadvantages, and also talking to me about some of their darker sides and crueler aspects. Just like in a blacksmith's forge, in order to keep me going, she would blow the bellows, wield the hammer, and strike the anvil. Her worst horror was reserved for anyone who didn't work. She pronounced the word "idle" in such a way as to utterly revile those to whom it applied. Her engagement book indicated the nature of her activities. It lay open on her table like a bible and was scribbled all over with different kinds of notations. If one had collected these pages over a twenty-year period and knew how to decipher them, one would have been able to figure out how she had spent her whole life. These memoranda of frivolous social activities and charitable occupations constituted a vast, mysterious network whose only function was to assist my father. Every tunnel was painstakingly maintained in the cunning windings of this anthill surrounding us. Indeed, her efforts were characterized by the tenacity of an ant. The crossed-out addresses on her calendar were not simply those of dead people but paths she had inadvertently strayed down that led nowhere and abandoned as soon as she realized her mistake.

I later learned what it cost her to keep up these connections and schemes when I understood the meaning of her frequent sighs in front of the mirror as she combed her graying hair or put a veil over her pale, worn face.

"Ah, that dinner at the Cottinis'. . ." she would let slip. "That call on Mme. Magnot . . ."

Cottini, the publisher of a famous newspaper, had the notorious reputation of being a "high liver," and Magnot, the deputy, had, it was whispered, lived with his mistress for several years before marrying her. My mother judged morals according to a rigorous and inflexible code.

Having learned from experience, my mother wished to keep me away from any career subject to intrigue or political influence. For other reasons, such as those of uncertain success or lack of discipline, she avoided liberal professions or those that depend on misconceptions.

"It's throwing yourself into the unknown," she used to say. "Wisdom in our day and age consists of joining a big private company where one knows the chairman. You tow the line, it's true, but without risking anything, and if you're intelligent and conscientious, as you are, you'll get ahead quickly while the rest will stay where they are."

Thus, although she would have regarded with distrust frequent visits to the magnificent house of the Montclars, "those idlers," she was very pleased with my close friendship with Philippe Robin, the lawyer's son. She lost no time in establishing a relationship with my friend's parents; on returning home from her visits to them, she would generally tell me that "all the smartest people of the Parisian bourgeoisie were there."

The friendship between Philippe Robin and myself wasn't based on our similar natures. Phillipe had a positive outlook on life; he was outgoing and laughed a lot. I, on the other hand, spoke seldom, was quite serious, and was particularly sensitive to things of the imagination. We were different, but we were particularly different as far as our moral values went, if that's how you would describe what mattered to a boy of less than fifteen.

When Philippe wanted something desperately, or gave in to some temptation, his actions were completely transparent. He hid nothing; he behaved frankly and carelessly, with the comfortable assurance of someone whose faults would be forgiven. That was not the case with me. I was always afraid that any deviation of conduct from "the straight and narrow path" that my high standards dictated would lead me permanently astray. Having grown up in an atmosphere loaded with the idea of the "thunderbolts" of the law, I was equally afraid of public opinion. Conscientious scruples and a cringing respect for higher authority restrained my actions and led me to put self-denial and caution ahead of other priorities. I felt successful when, thanks to some hypocritical dissimulation on my part, I was able to dampen any curiosity about my behavior. What a feeling of triumph when I managed to stifle some dubious impulse I couldn't resist the pleasure of artificially provoking.

I sometimes allowed myself evil thoughts and gave them free rein to develop in my imagination; I delighted in my excitement and then, in a sudden burst of intense passion, I would get rid of these so-called unhealthy ideas. This gave me the noble feeling of having strengthened my character. It was just like at Aiguesbelles, where my grandfather gave orders in the spring that certain vine stocks not be pruned, so that when strolling around his property he himself would have the satisfaction of handling the clippers. He bent over the dangerously neglected stock, clipping and snipping with thoughtful intensity, and then, drawing himself up, would say to me proudly, "You see, my boy, the best vine is that which is most carefully pruned."

CHAPTER

2

I was seated next to Silbermann in English class and therefore could observe him at leisure. Silbermann was so attentive to every word the professor said that his eyes never left the teacher's face. His pointed chin jutted out and his pendulous lips hung down, his features appeared curiously taut, and only the Adam's apple sticking out from his neck moved from time to time. His slightly animal-like profile, strangely lit by the sunlight in the classroom, reminded me of the lizards on the terrace at Aiguesbelles who, in the heat of the day, would come out of every nook and cranny, heads jutting forward and throats pumping, to survey the human race.

DE LACRETELLE : SILBERMANN

A good deal of the English class was spent in practicing conversation. Silbermann, eagerly raising his hand, repeatedly asked to speak. He was much more fluent than the rest of us. We didn't exchange a word during these two hours. He ignored me completely, although once I caught a fearful look from him. In any case, he behaved that way toward everyone those first few days. But this was probably due to suspicion rather than timidity, because after some time we could see that he had selected two or three rather meek boys whom he would approach as soon as he had spotted them and, with a commanding air, would then lecture them loudly and confidently.

He never played during recess. He appeared to disdain strength and agility and would walk through groups of boys playing games without the slightest sign of interest. But if a discussion was going on, he always noticed and stopped right away, no matter what the subject was. One sensed that he was dying to give his opinion, as if he possessed a superabundance of intellectual energy.

He mostly sought out the company of the teachers. When the drumroll announced the short break between classes and we all shot outdoors, he would often sidle up to the teacher's desk and initiate a conversation by asking some clever question. From his perch on the platform, he would watch us come in with a look of pride. I admired him at these moments, thinking how embarrassed I would have been in his place. It was soon obvious that not only was Silbermann capable of remaining in tenth grade, but that he would probably be near the top of the class. His grades, from the outset, were excellent, and he deserved them as much for his knowledge as for his hard work. He seemed gifted with an extraordinary memory and always knew the lessons without a single mistake. This was a source of amazement to me because, as an average student, I had great difficulty remembering mine. I was completely dense when it came to schoolwork; the words seemed shrouded in some kind of uniform gray matter that prevented me from distinguishing between them and grasping their meaning. One day, however, the veil was torn away, and new light was shed on my subjects of study. This happened thanks to Silbermann.

It was during French class. We had prepared the first scene of *Iphigénie*.* Silbermann stood up when called on and began to recite:

> *Yes, it is I, Agamemnon, your King, who wakens you.*
> *Come and do recognize my voice that strikes against your ear.*

Most of the good students recited the verses in a subdued monotone, and Silbermann didn't declaim them with emphasis, but his diction nonetheless remained natural. His subtle delivery was so confident and so unpedantic that we were all amazed. Some of us smiled, but I was absolutely transfixed and struck by a sudden revelation. These collections of words, which I rec-

*Names and titles that are asterisked appear in *Notes* (see page 155).

ognized because I had seen them in print and had committed them to memory, one by one, now formed for the first time an impression on my mind. I slowly began to realize that they expressed a reality and made sense in everyday life. As Silbermann continued and I listened to the sound of his voice, ideas sprang up in my mind as in a soil that had remained barren until then. Scenes from *Iphigénie* began to take form as scenes from reality that in no way resembled those I had seen in the theater with painted scenery and artificial light. I envisioned a camp by the shore of a river; the waves, which no wind stirred, gently lapped on the sand; there among the shadowy tents in a soundless dawn, two thoughtful-looking men conversed.

I would not have believed possible such a living, vibrant conception of a classical tragedy. I could not have been more moved if a marble statue had come to life. I looked at the person who had made all this happen. Silbermann had gone over his time limit and still continued his recitation. His eyes sparkled and his lips glistened as if he had just eaten some delectable morsel.

The teacher, upon hearing a few of the students grumbling about Silbermann's overenthusiasm, cut him off and congratulated him. Silbermann sat down. He was happy. I realized that from the slight quiver of his nostrils. But didn't this breath rather belong, I asked myself, to the soul of some mysterious genius who dwelt within him? This idea appealed to my childish imagination, which still inclined toward the fantastic; and as I stared at him until almost hypnotized, he conjured up in my mind, with his sallow complexion and his frizzy cap of black hair, a magician from some oriental fable who holds the key to every wonder.

We spoke to each other several days later, one Sunday morning, under circumstances I vividly remember. I had been to church with my mother, and coming out, I left her. I always felt somewhat excited after the service since I took great pleasure in expending my exaltation on profane things. I liked to walk alone in the Bois de Boulogne, full of emotion, with the sound of the organ still humming in my ear, thrilled with the joyfulness of the Psalms. In this state of spiritual intoxication, I liked to give myself over to physical activities: running, jumping over bushes, drinking in the smell of the leaves and the earth. I put myself in touch with living nature. Then, looking up to the sky, I stopped, not suddenly calmer, but as though struck by a burst of loving feeling. The sight of a cloud floating in the blue of the sky awakened my heart and my imagination. Shaking, I yearned for the sweetest and noblest of consciousness and dreamt of all the adventures it would bring. This feeling often crystallized into a bonding where, in a mystical alliance, an intellectual link and the idea of total devotion mingled together indistinctly.

Still reeling from my confused state of mind that morning in Ranelagh Park,* I saw Silbermann coming toward me. He was alone. He took short, hurried steps, frequently shaking his head, as though he were full of disturbing thoughts or felt that he was being pursued. He saw me from a distance but made no sign of recognition and, instead, opened a book he had in his hand. Just as he was about to pass, he looked at me hesitatingly and smiled slightly; when I responded with a very cordial hello, his expression suddenly changed, and he came toward me, expressing his delight at our meeting.

"Do you live near here? Whereabouts?"

He wanted to know the name of the street, the number of the house; he asked me about my habits, my family—all in such a natural, friendly manner that I took pleasure in answering the questions, despite my normal reticence.

"Where are you headed?" he added. "Shall I keep you company?"

I accepted. He showed me his book.

"It's an early edition of Ronsard.* I just bought it," he said, caressing the lovely binding with his thin brown fingers. He opened the book and began to read me some lines. I had the same sensation as in class. The lines as read by him seemed full of something I longed to taste. The words took on new qualities: they flattered my senses; they aroused an unknown emotion and a sort of vibration in my brain. But what can I say about Silbermann himself, and how can I describe his face? He read these lines:

> *Mow down, my boy, with your plundering hands*
> *The gorgeous luster of the green season*
> *Then with full fists strew the house*
> *With the flowers that April begets in its youth.*

His nostrils dilated, as though pricked by the pungent odor of hay, and tears of pleasure filled his eyes. We had arrived at a corner of lawn where a statue of La Fontaine* stood. Silbermann pointed to it and indignantly said, "Can you imagine anything more hideous than this bust with a Muse crowning it? And the group of animals—the lion, the fox, and the crow—what a banal composition. This is the only way we know how to honor a great man. But other ways do exist. Last summer I was in Weimar and visited Goethe's house, which has been preserved intact. Not a single object in his room has been touched since his death. In the town—and with what respect!—they show the bench on which he sat, the summer house where he used to go to dream. I can assure you, such memorials have grandeur. You don't see anything like that in France. A few years ago, the château of St. Point in Burgundy, where Lamartine* lived, was sold. Well, my father was able to buy many objects that had belonged to Lamartine; and, by the way, it turned out to be an excellent business deal."

We were still standing in front of the statue.

"Do you like La Fontaine?" he asked me.

As the question embarrassed me, he went on enthusiastically, "My dear boy, it's quite simple: La Fontaine is our greatest portrayer of manners. In his fables, which we are taught to mimic, he describes his whole century. Louis XIV and his court, the bourgeoisie and the peasants of his time; that's what we should be looking for behind all his animals. That's when you see the wisdom behind the anecdote and the boldness of his morality and it's what Taine* understood so well. Have you read his book *La Fontaine and His Fables*?

I shook my head.

"I'll lend it to you."

I didn't answer. I was stunned. This boy who owned rare books and who made confident distinctions: "this is beautiful . . . that is not"; who had traveled, read, observed, retained impressions, threw such a variety of wonderful ideas at me that I was dumbfounded. I looked at him. I didn't doubt that he was unquestionably superior to all my friends and not at all comparable to anyone in my family or any of the other people I knew. His passion for intellectual subjects and his gifted way of making accessible what had seemed beyond one's grasp were for me truly new qualities. And who in my circle could speak both so powerfully and so gently, in a way that both impressed and charmed?

He hadn't stopped talking, continuing to cite the names of writers and titles of books.

I had immense respect for everything about literature. I placed certain writers who had aroused my imagination above the rest of humankind, just like the gods of Olympus. Silbermann acquainted me with many hitherto unknown facts, referring easily to one and then another. He finally revealed that "le père Hugo" was his god. I listened avidly. I don't know if it was his air of familiarity, his tone of voice, or his sallow complexion, but at that moment I envisioned a scene that made me slightly draw back.

A swarthy Spanish fruit seller would often pass by on the road at Aiguesbelles and stop his cart in front of the farmhouse, crying out his wares in a strange voice and roughly handling his beautiful red apples, his tender dusky peaches, his smooth glossy plums. Celestine, our

cook, disliked this man "who came from goodness knows where," and when she had finished
dealing with him, one could hear her back in the
kitchen grumbling, "What a shame to see lovely
fruit touched by hands like that."

Silbermann, unaware of my instinctive shudder, continued, "If the books interest you, come
over to my house someday and I'll show you anything you like."

I thanked him and accepted the invitation.

"Well, when would you like to come?" he immediately rejoined. "Are you free this afternoon?"

I was not, but he insisted.

"Come for tea next Thursday."

There was something about his eagerness that
I disliked and that put me on the defensive. I
replied that we'd set the day later. Since we had
arrived at my parents' house, I held out my hand.
Silbermann took it and held it and, looking at
me with gratitude, said in an infinitely gentle
voice, "I am glad, very glad, that we met ... I
didn't think we could be friends."

"And why is that?" I asked him with genuine surprise.

"At school I always used to see you with Robin and since he refused to speak to me for a whole month this summer, I thought that you, too . . . Even in English class, where we sit next to each other, I didn't dare . . ."

He no longer seemed as confident when he spoke. His voice was low and broken; it seemed to rise up from secret and sorrowful depths. His hand, which continued to grasp mine as if he wished to attach himself to me, shook a little. I was completely upset by his tone and by his shaking. I sensed in this human being, so different from others, a persistent and incurable secret sadness, like that of an orphan or a person with some infirmity.

Pretending not to have understood, I smiled and stammered: "But that's absurd . . . For whatever reason did you suppose . . ."

"Because I am Jewish," he interrupted sharply in such a peculiar tone of voice that I couldn't tell if the admission was painful to him or whether he was proud of it. Confused by my tactlessness and wanting to make amends, I desperately searched for the most gentle words I could think of. But in my family I had never been taught tenderness. The only sign of affection shown was some sacrifice offered under difficult circumstances, and that had value only when inspired by conscience.

So, stepping back and still holding Silbermann's hand, I solemnly said to him, "I swear, Silbermann, that from now on I will do everything in my power for you."

The same day, I spent the afternoon at Philippe Robin's. Toward evening, Philippe's uncle Marc le Hellier arrived. He was very fond of his nephew and treated him like a man, not a schoolboy, which flattered Philippe. He liked to say to him that nothing was more absurd than the education given in the lycées, that a fencing match developed the brain better than studying, and that knowing just where to deliver a knockout punch was more useful in life than anything we were taught.

He took up the theme again, seeing Philippe's thick textbooks on the table. He made a back-handed gesture, as if to shove them onto the floor, and Philippe burst out laughing. It reminded me of Silbermann touching the Ronsard book and his fiery intensity when he recited a poem.

"Do you know where I was a little while ago, Philippe?" said Marc le Hellier. "At the first Frenchmen for France* meeting since the beginning of autumn. We're not doing so badly! Almost five hundred new members in three months. Now we can act."

Philippe looked very interested. His uncle had pulled him over to feel his arm, and I noticed that Philippe proudly flexed his biceps.

"First," continued le Hellier, "we are going to organize a campaign against the Jews that, I can tell you, will be carefully and intelligently conducted. Not the old street demonstrations, which have been fine so far. No, we are going to start setting up files and dossiers; and as Jewish fortunes are usually based on dubious dealings, we'll follow the tracks of every Jew we suspect and then at the right moment—*pht!*—we'll break his back."

He made a sharp gesture with his hand. Under the thick, closely clipped red moustache, his upper lip curled, revealing a huge pair of wicked-looking canines.

I didn't like this man at all, with his coarse and excessive leanings, who tried to influence Philippe and distanced him from me. But on this particular day I listened to his plans with a real sense of distress. I seemed to hear Silbermann's lamentation from afar—"I thought you'd refuse to talk to me . . . I didn't dare . . ."—so that soon afterwards, as Philippe's uncle continued talking and Philippe, his eyes shining, hung on every word, I got up and left.

Silbermann's appeal to my pity had touched

me deeply. I thought about him the whole evening, feeling even more attracted than when I had been merely dazzled by his marvelous gifts. I remembered his fearful look that first day and the reason for his hesitation in approaching me that morning; as these images became clear, I was profoundly shaken by the picture of Silbermann as an outcast among us.

In my room, I automatically picked up one of my notebooks and opened it toward the end. There, on those scribbled pages, my secrets could be found; in this book I would begin a confession, write an imaginary friend, or scrawl girls' names. Later, when I realized the childishness of these things, or blushed with shame at the disturbing daydreams they evoked, I hastily erased everything I'd written.

I wrote to Silbermann and assured him he was quite wrong in thinking that I would treat him as Robin had, since I bore no hostility toward his race. I also slipped in the fact that I was a Protestant. I added that I had thought about our meeting all day and that I would never forget the oath of friendship I had sworn as we parted.

I did not intend to give him this letter. However, in school the following day, as he ran up to me full of affectionate greetings, I abruptly tore the page out of my notebook, folded it up, and handed it to him.

I spent the next recess with Robin. To my great embarrassment, I saw Silbermann coming up to us. He said to me in a very loud voice, "It's understood, then, and I'll count on you for Thursday." Then he walked away.

Philippe looked at me with surprise. "You're going out together on Thursday? How do you know him?"

Blushing deeply, I explained that I had run into him and he had offered to lend me some books.

"You know that his father is an antique dealer and a thief. My uncle Marc told me so."

This warning was pronounced severely. I gestured vaguely, and we went on to some other topic.

What happened the next day was like an omen of the troubled times to come.

It was Saint Barbara's feast day. On that date, students preparing for advanced studies in science would organize a noisy disturbance that was winked at by the school authorities. The lower grades were not involved, but it created a certain feeling of excitement throughout the school.

That year, the uproar was tremendous. As afternoon classes were ending, the light of Bengal fires suddenly lit up the whole courtyard and then went out again. Shouting and singing broke out. A second later, a loud explosion made us jump. A suppressed excitement ran though the room. I looked nervously at the dark windows, disgusted by this savage riot. The drum sounded. The boys rushed to the door, shouting, and one of them, I don't know who, ran in front of Silbermann and, shoving him back, yelled ferociously in his face, "Death to the Jews!"

CHAPTER

3

Silbermann's parents lived in a beautiful new house bordering on the Parc de la Muette. The apartment, on the top floor, was huge. Silbermann showed me around, stopping me in front of magnificent marquetry furniture and lighting the paintings. I had never been in a house full of so many valuable objects. I looked out the windows. One could see only the tall, superb trees of the park and, in the distance, an undulating line of hills—the countryside. As the sun's rays filtered through the windows, I had the impression that golden veils had been draped around everything. It could have been a view from a country château. I went around wordlessly, unable to speak, so deep was my feeling of humility. I thought of my father's study over the courtyard, narrow and austere, and of my mother's small sitting room where the mostly rustic antiques, chosen from Aiguesbelles, were its finest decoration.

Luckily, Silbermann, who showed me these things as modestly as possible, didn't prolong my discomfort and took me to his room. This was quite different and I felt a slight twinge of satisfaction, saying to myself, "I like mine better." As a matter of fact, the room was so modest that it didn't in any way follow those I had just seen. On closer examination, I thought to myself that my mother would undoubtedly have worked her fingers to the bone rather than allow me to sleep amidst the disorder that reigned there.

Silbermann pointed out the bookcase that covered almost an entire wall.

"Look," he said.

There were books from floor to ceiling: some were richly bound, while others were dog-eared paperbacks.

"Are these yours? Have you read all that?" I exclaimed with admiration.

"Yes," said Silbermann with a little smile of pride. And he added, "I bet all those St. Xavier boys together haven't read half of them, huh?"

He showed me them in detail, handling certain volumes carefully and explaining what made them rare. He opened several and, with an assuredness and a sense of appropriateness, read me a selection of extraordinary passages. He interrupted himself a few times, saying with moist eyes, "Isn't this beautiful? And listen to this next one . . ." He was particularly sensitive to form or, rather, to the word that creates an image; he would emphasize it with a gesture of his hand as if the wonders of the mind were like clay he was attempting to model.

The book and the printed word held an irresistible attraction for me. Here in this library (so different from my father's, which comprised works of fact, not designed to touch the imagination), I turned the pages of these books with emotion and plied Silbermann with questions. He had the gift of summing up in a sentence the subject of a book, reducing it succinctly.

"*Les Misérables*,"* he replied to one of my questions, "is the epic of the people." Then, as he handed me a slim volume on the back cover of which I read, *Oeuvres de Paul-Louis Courier*,* "This is the vocabulary of the French language."

I was filled with admiration for his vast knowledge and quick judgment. Silbermann sensed this and, smiling, said to me, "Take whatever you'd like. You can come here as often as you please."

We had a long conversation. He gave me advice about my studies. We talked about our fellow classmates, and he made clever fun of some who were generally considered idiots. He often dwelled on a word he seemed to adore—"intelligence"—and pronounced it so forcefully that little balls of spit formed in the corners of his lips.

I mentioned several books I had read, and he gave me new insights into each one. We were sitting side by side; the inflections of his voice sometimes seemed to hypnotize me.

He introduced me to his mother. She was going out and was wrapped in a long fur coat down to her ankles. All I could glimpse of her face were almond-shaped black eyes and very red lips that never stopped smiling. She reproached her son for keeping me in his room rather than in one of the drawing rooms. She invited me to lunch, set the day, and disappeared, having charmed me with her elegance and cordiality.

Just before leaving, I went to choose several books from Silbermann's library. In looking through a row I saw hidden at the back a stack of newspapers. My eye caught a title: *La Sion Future*.

At about this time, the hostility toward Silbermann broke out at school.

He had twice come out first in composition, and this success had aroused jealousy among the better students. But the animosity soon became general.

Things started off with fairly innocent teasing when Silbermann began to declaim and gesture. Silbermann aggravated this teasing by his resistance and encouraged it by his insistence on always having the last word. Our teachers also added fuel to the fire through their indifference to the situation, for, despite Silbermann's doing well, they did not like him. It became very noticeable the day one of them, annoyed at his constantly coming up to the desk, sent him away with a rude and stinging comment that everyone overheard.

Soon during break it became a popular amusement to surround Silbermann, make fun of him, and rough him up. As soon as he appeared, boys would say, "Hey, there's Silbermann. Let's give him a hard time."

They would shove him, snatch off his cap, and throw his books on the ground. Silbermann didn't defend himself physically but would make a sarcastic remark that more often than not hit home and exasperated his aggressors. Initially, these little verbal victories gave him so much pleasure that he forgot about his detractors and even invited their malice. But I came to realize that he was beginning to suffer as these scenes repeated themselves and as his odd appearance exposed him to a general curiosity. Finally, a short time later, when the St. Xavier boys joined in, the game took on the nature of a real persecution.

The St. Xavierites basically did not take part in our school life. Great lords, obligated to spend time in a place unworthy of them, they considered it pointless to establish relationships with neighbors who were there by chance. Each little squad would march directly to its place, pretending to see and hear nothing. Their attitude toward the teachers was generally polite but never enthusiastic; their real masters were those they would see again after leaving the lycée.

DE LACRETELLE : SILBERMANN

Sometimes in class, the expression on the face of a boy like Montclar betrayed a feeling worse than rebelliousness; it was as if he had an ancient score to settle with the man who taught him.

It was Montclar who changed the nature of the harassment toward Silbermann. He was the first to attack him about his physical characteristics and the practices of his religion. Montclar, who wasn't witty, had a kind of cruel impetuosity and fiery energy that completely subdued Silbermann. The rest, whose convictions were perhaps weaker than Montclar's but who were flattered by his presence among them, followed suit. No opportunity for insulting Silbermann was overlooked. And so during our study of *Esther*,* where the Jews were mentioned everywhere, he had to endure the sight of twenty malicious faces turned toward him. There were two other Jewish boys in the class—Haase, the son of a banker whose sister had married a d'Anthenay, and Crémieux, whose father was a deputy—but they were not bothered. Neither was as pronounced a Semitic type as Silbermann. Haase tried to erase his Jewish characteristics by assuming British habits: he plastered down his hair to unfrizz it and spoke with an affected accent. They both seemed to consider themselves superior to Silbermann.

It was extremely painful for me to see Philippe join the persecutors. I certainly knew that he enjoyed slightly violent games, and I also knew that he was influenced by the behavior of a Montclar or a La Béchellière, but his kindness had always prevented him from acting in a way that would actually hurt another person. I couldn't explain this obstinate, deep-seated hatred toward Silbermann. Philippe seemed to feel his life and property were in danger.

I arrived at Silbermann's for lunch and was introduced to his father, a slightly heavyset man. A foreign accent slowed down his speech, and his lifeless eyes, yellowish flesh, stubby beard, and thick nose and lips all gave his face a loutish, sleepy look. But occasionally he would break into the conversation with a remark that showed he was awake.

Just as I had originally thought, Mme. Silbermann was fairly pretty with fine features. All the same, her smile was so charming, so youthful, and so frequent that ultimately it made her expression seem insincere. Her gestures were quick and dainty, but a rather fleshy swelling below the nape of her neck made her seem less graceful.

Silbermann's role as a son was entirely different from mine. He was asked his advice, and he also had the right to ask questions or disagree and completely join in the conversation. He was treated like a young king. On the other hand, Mme. Silbermann did not appear to share her husband's interests in the slightest. This was so very different from what I was accustomed to that they seemed less like three members of a family than like members of an association or a tribe.

I was treated with a respect to which I was entirely unaccustomed. M. Silbermann inquired after my father, "the great magistrate," and Mme. Silbermann told me she had often seen my mother at charity events. These subjects of conversation displeased their son, who not only interrupted them but even became rude. When our future careers were discussed, he declared that he would devote himself to literature. While his mother appeared to approve, his father shook his head and said pleasantly, "No, no, David, that's not serious."

"Why not, Father?" cried Silbermann animatedly. "I could never do the same things as you: they wouldn't interest me."

"Oh, antiques," said M. Silbermann gently. "There's not much future in that now that people in society are going 'into the trade,' but there are other profitable fields. If I were twenty years old, I'd head to America with a stock of pearls."

His son didn't conceal a look of contempt.

After lunch, Silbermann offered to take me to

the theater. I wasn't very enthusiastic because when I was with him, I liked nothing better than to hear him talk. And so we went for a walk in the Bois de Boulogne. I immediately turned the conversation around to my favorite subject: literature. This, for me, was like one of those exotic places that mysteriously attract you and set you to dreaming. Silbermann knew the whole park intimately and where the best views were; he guided me there and helped me to distinguish what exactly made the landscape beautiful. Sometimes, taking me by the arm, he would stop me as if exclaiming, "Look at this silver river and all these mountains" and then recite a couple of lines of poetry or some magnificent phrase. I felt transported and wished he would go on forever. And just as I would have asked the traveler describing the Pyramids to me, "And the Nile?" when Silbermann had taught me everything he knew about a writer I would ask, "And Vigny?*... and Chateaubriand?*" Then, indefatigable, he'd be off again, his mind quick and confident, like an explorer whose memory and enthusiasm never flag.

After strolling a long time, we arrived at the edge of a little lake.

"Chateaubriand, Hugo . . ." murmured Silbermann dreamily, "to be one of them! And possess their gifts and play their part: that's what I should like.

"Oh, no!" he continued. "I have no intention of selling furniture or pearls. My ambition is very different. I want to devote all my abilities and everything I have here," he said, touching his forehead, "to the service of literature." Then, lowering his voice, "If they knew that, maybe they would torment me less? . . ."

He was alluding to the horrible treatment he endured at school. I felt how terribly he suffered and searched everywhere for a subject to distract him.

We were alone. It was one of the last days of autumn, cold and sad. Heavy clouds covered the sky, and the dark waters of the lake rippled. The trees were bare; only the green from a clump of fir trees remained. This pitiful bit of greenery that survived, surrounded by dead woods, made me think of life: miserable and eternal.

We stopped.

"Listen," said Silbermann, in a voice that had become a little hoarse. "My father settled in France thirty years ago. His father lived in Germany but came from Poland. About the others, further back, I know nothing except that they must have lived like all the people of their race: ashamed and persecuted. But I do know that I was born in France and I want to stay here. I want to break away from that kind of nomadic life and free myself from the hereditary destiny that makes most of us vagabonds.

"Oh! I'm not going to deny my origins," he declared, with that little quiver of the nostrils that revealed his pride. "On the contrary, I can't imagine more favorable circumstances in which to accomplish great things than to be both a Jew and a Frenchman." He raised his finger prophetically. "But I want to shape the genius of my race according to the character of this country; I want to unite my resources with yours, and if I write, I don't want to be criticized for being in any way 'a foreigner.' I don't want to hear about anything I write the comment, 'It's certainly Jewish.' So you see, I intend to use my intelligence, my tenacity, and all my gifts to know deeply and thoroughly this cultural heritage that, although not mine, I may perhaps add to one day. I want to make it mine."

He emphasized this last sentence, tapping the ground with his foot.

"Is that impossible? Can't I understand these things as well as Montclar or Robin? Tell me, don't I appreciate them more than they do? And whom do I harm? There is no secret plot or selfish motive in my ambition. Why won't they have anything to do with me? And why do they hate me so?"

He talked while I stared straight ahead. He spoke with such power that everything I knew about Israel's trials seemed to pass before my eyes against the unforgiving background of the autumn landscape. I pictured a small lake in Judea, like this one, from whose shores the Jews one day had set forth. I had a vision of these Jews wandering around the earth down through the ages, encamped on wasteland in the countryside, or tolerated in cities only within certain limits and forced to wear degrading clothes. Oppressed everywhere, avoiding punishment by enduring injury, they consoled themselves for the terrible treatment men inflicted on them by worshipping an ever more terrible god. And at the end of these generations burdened with hardship, I saw Silbermann, who had taken refuge by my side. Pitiful, eyes darting with an uneasy look, and often agitated by odd movements, he seemed to feel deeply the pain of all the wanderings and miseries endured by his ancestors. And now finally he wished to rest among us. By joining with us, he wanted to leave behind the scars that persecution and a nomadic life had stamped upon his race. He offered us his love and his strength. But this alliance was pushed away and confronted with a universal hatred.

I was extremely moved at the thought of such devastating images and abominable injustice. It seemed to me that Silbermann's voice, simple and poignant, rose among the endless voices of martyrs. He said, "Tomorrow I shall be insulted and beaten . . . Is that just?" And he held out his two bare palms, just as the figure of Christ is shown among his enemies.

CHAPTER

4

This scene greatly troubled me. The next night, half awake and half asleep, I dreamt about the biblical image it had evoked. In the morning, I felt that a duty had been thrust upon me: to redeem humankind's injustice to Silbermann, I must not only love him, but I must side with him against everyone, no matter how difficult and bleak the task. Besides, weren't his main enemies the St. Xavier boys, and hadn't I always felt, except for Philippe Robin, a natural animosity toward them? I decided to speak to Philippe in an attempt to separate him from Silbermann's enemies.

I sought him out that same day. I pointed out

the cruelty of the treatment inflicted on Silbermann. "I know he suffers a great deal," I added.
And I appealed to Philippe's good heart to
stop it.

"I, too, have something to say on the subject,"
he answered. "It's extremely unpleasant for me
to have one of my friends associate with that
boy."

"And why is that?" I asked.

"Why?. . . Because he's a Jew."

This was the identical reason given by Silbermann. Philippe had spoken harshly, and I felt
that this argument was conclusive for him.
While searching for something conciliatory to
say, I gestured rather carelessly.

"Oh! I know," Philippe went on. "Quite possibly it's of no importance to you people." His
superior tone and his reference to my Protestantism hurt me deeply.

"At least *we others* don't falsify the word of
God," I said, my voice shaking.

Philippe lightly shrugged his shoulders. "In

any case," he declared, "you must choose between him and me."

I suddenly thought of everything Philippe's friendship meant to me—gentle and moderated feelings, easy and approved pleasures—and I almost abandoned Silbermann then. But, on the other hand, I was given a difficult challenge and foresaw a painful road ahead. Excited by the prospect of sacrifice, I took a deep breath to give me strength and answered: "Him."

We parted.

From then on, I devoted myself entirely to Silbermann. I ran to join him at every recess, hoping to protect him by my presence. Luckily, with the arrival of winter, his situation somewhat eased: because of the cold, we remained in our classroom, where no one dared to do anything against him. In the evening, when school let out, we escaped under cover of darkness.

On the street, we would walk together, and I would accompany him to his door. Sometimes I went upstairs with him, and we would do our homework. I was amazed at how easily and well he studied. When doing a Latin translation, he would first quickly read the sentence with a tense look; then he would think for a few seconds, feverishly biting his lips; finally, he would read it, moving his head and hands to the rhythm of the words and, hardly consulting the dictionary, he would write the translation. Sitting opposite him, completely uninspired and searching carefully for the meaning of each word, I would go forward step by step, completely in the dark.

When we were finished, we would go to the library, where he would share his latest discovery with me. Not a week went by that he wasn't enthusiastic about a new work. It was an extravagant enthusiasm that would lead me suddenly from a sonnet of The Pleiades* to a tale by Voltaire or a chapter by Michelet.* He would take up the book and read. He would often hold my arm and grip it hard when we got to the passages he particularly admired. He never wanted to stop, and he once read aloud in its entirety the "Conversation of the Marshal d'Hocquincourt,"* acting out in turn the different accents and comical expressions of the Jesuit father, the Jansenist, and the Marshal.

Soon we spent all our free days together, and it was he who decided how they should be spent. I never objected to his plans and sacrificed my wishes to his without regret. Wasn't it up to me to devote myself completely to his happiness, thereby redeeming the acts of the wicked? When it was difficult to agree, I would repeat to myself, "It's my mission," which resigned me to any disappointment. Nonetheless, while following his lead, I tried to inadvertently guide him as well. My mission was to rid him of certain unpleasant characteristics by slowly reforming him bit by bit. I hadn't entirely figured out the extent of this plan, but we would sometimes deliberately walk past the little Protestant church in Passy. I never said a word and didn't even point it out, but somewhere in my mind lurked the idea that perhaps I would take him there.

I had spoken about him to my parents. They wanted to meet him, so I invited him to lunch. My mother, who was sensitive and horrified by violence, was very moved by my description of Silbermann's treatment at school. My mother's feelings toward Jews were difficult to determine. Brought up in a country where Catholics and Protestants are still deeply opposed, she sympathized with the Jews as a fellow minority. Besides, she was careful not to dismiss their support of my father's career and relied on many connections in Jewish circles. But I actually had noticed that she became, oh, almost imperceptibly, standoffish when she found herself with one of them. Another observation, made entirely by chance, further enlightened me.

In a certain neighborhood of Nîmes—which we often visited from Aiguesbelles—stood a house known as "the house of the Jew." Built on

a peculiar axis, it was very conspicuous, and
when we went by, my mother never failed to tell
me about the history and habits of the family
who used to live there. There was never the
slightest contempt or tinge of sarcasm in what
she said, but her words conveyed the same impression of secrecy and distrust she had when,
avoiding a place full of garbage and ash heaps a
little further on at the town gates, she would say,
"That's the gypsies' campground." This explains
my reluctance to bring Silbermann home; I
couldn't predict what his reception would be
and, as will be seen, I wasn't wrong.

I was down in the drawing room when he arrived. He examined everything very closely.
Spotting a book on my mother's desk, he turned
it over to see the title. I remember it was Amiel's
Journal intime.* Silbermann gave a little smile
that, I can't explain why, I didn't like. He
greeted my parents with the utmost respect, but
as soon as our conversation was launched, I felt
uncomfortable. He rattled on at the slightest

hint of a question, in what I am sure my father considered the worst possible taste. He continued during lunch, telling all kinds of stories in which he appeared to advantage: his reading, his travels, his goals . . . I saw my mother look at him askance, as if she suspected some diabolical motive in all this feverish intellectual activity.

My father remained monosyllabic during the meal.

The most amazing thing was that his animation, which usually delighted me, sounded offensive instead. Silbermann, in his desire to shine, came up with outlandish stories and absurd opinions. And nothing was more shocking than the effect his words had in an atmosphere where I had previously heard only measured advice and generally accepted opinions. I wished I could signal him to stop because listening to him was so physically painful that my hands were clenched, but he didn't seem to have the slightest doubt about the impression he made. My mother and father gave him forced smiles, and he in turn addressed himself to each polite listener.

I was relieved when the meal ended. My father retired to his study where, later, Silbermann came to say good-bye. He examined the bookcases, full of law books and judicial catalogues, and said, "As La Rochefoucauld wrote, isn't the concept of justice born from our great fear of being deprived of that which belongs to us?"

My father, with icy courtesy, made a noncommittal gesture.

That evening, my mother said, "Your friend seems very intelligent," in the same tone of voice one might describe a swindler as being very ingenious. This singular lack of success did not lower Silbermann in my esteem. It was only proof of certain limitations on the part of my family. My environment seemed narrow and confined, incapable of giving intelligence a large part. Little habits, to which I had always submitted, now seemed ridiculous. I also noticed that many of our belongings, so familiar I had never considered them, were extremely ugly. I took less pleasure in being home and, either for this reason or for fear that Silbermann would notice my parents' dislike, I arranged for him to visit as seldom as possible.

Our relationship didn't suffer. On the contrary, it seemed my company was indispensable to Silbermann, and he took me everywhere. On Sundays we generally went to the theater. As soon as the curtain fell, he would peremptorily praise or criticize the actors and the play, which would settle my own uncertain opinions. On Thursdays we would go to some bookstore, where he would discuss the different editions and bindings; he would bargain, buy, or make a trade. He always had plenty of pocket money, and I often blushed at his generosity to me on our outings. At the end of the day, after writing down my expenses—a habit inculcated in me by my father—I would amuse myself trying to calculate how much he had spent and discovering it was large amounts.

DE LACRETELLE : SILBERMANN

Our conversations were not always about art or literature. He followed political events and social movements with just as much interest and enjoyed discussing them.

One day he took me to an out-of-the-way neighborhood where a popular demonstration was being held. He wore a red rosette in his buttonhole and spoke familiarly to people around him. Terrified, I followed him through the mob and quickly begged him to turn back. On our return we passed a square in Montmartre with a magnificent view of Paris and stopped. The sight of the city at his feet seemed to strangely excite Silbermann. In a declamatory voice, he expounded his theories and depicted our society in the future. He affirmed his belief in the betterment of humankind and in universal happiness. "These times will come," he cried, "as surely as the sun will rise tomorrow."

Intoxicated by this promise, I enthusiastically followed his finger pointing toward the city to indicate what must be swept away and to show the plan for the new utopia. "Who will have the glory of assuring the material paradise of humankind?" he asked dreamily. And his eyes shone as if he had had a flash of insight that he could be this Messiah.

Thus the winter passed.

At school, Silbermann was as successful as ever, although he was often criticized for his lack of methodology. Our French teacher also reprimanded him for his reading errors and the skill with which he appropriated the ideas and style of others; he implied that this conduct, coming as it did from Silbermann, did not surprise him.

Spring marked the resumption of hostilities against Silbermann. Everyone took part in outdoor games with renewed energy. In the courtyard, the boys formed circles that would suddenly hold Silbermann prisoner. They made faces at his ugliness, which had become more and more striking because as he matured he lost the look of childish precocity that had given him a kind of grace. Constantly insulted and shoved

by new assailants, he savagely resisted, first
against one and then another, until, finally desperate and worn out, he would try to break the
circle and be thrown down.

Elections were held that year. People cam-
paigned furiously. Brightly colored posters plastered everywhere caught one's eye. We would
stop to read them and arrive at school stirred up
by party differences. The Frenchmen for France
league played an important role in the electoral
campaign and multiplied its attacks against the
Jews by means of proclamations, meetings, and
public rallies. Philippe Robin distributed anti-
Semitic badges and pamphlets, supplied by his
uncle, to anyone. This crusade found a victim in
Silbermann. His name was written and his caricature drawn next to the posters on the wall. Finally, Montclar organized a regular gang against
him at the school.

Montclar was a strange character. Most of
his cohorts from St. Xavier's, by virtue of their
spindly legs and pale hands and some distinctive

feature reminiscent of a sort of heraldic emblem—a bony flat nose, a narrow forehead, a feminine curve—seemed to belong to a decadent species. He stood out by virtue of his normal build and air of leadership.

He also had a leader's spirit. He picked out two or three boys from the most brutal, thuggish, and toadying types in our class and set them against Silbermann. Leading the gang, he would go toward Silbermann in the courtyard and, standing back several feet (since he pretended he couldn't go near such a vile creature), begin to insult him: "Jew, tell us when you're going back to your ghetto because we don't want you here . . . Jew, why have you got goat's ears?"

Silbermann, while showing signs of fear like those of a weak animal that knows it is being stalked, bravely answered back every word. Then, at a signal from Montclar, the others would hurl themselves at him, throw him to the ground, and beat him mercilessly. I tried to help him, but I was stopped and forcibly held back. I could see the fight going on from a distance. I heard Montclar egg on one of his mercenaries and then watched the boy acknowledge this favor by redoubling his brutality. I spotted Robin among the attackers. He didn't hit hard, and with his blond hair all mussed up, he was like a medieval page at his first call to battle. Our eyes often met, but he would turn away quickly as if to avoid the imploring look in mine. It was horrible for me to see the charm of this face, which I had loved not so long ago, harden into callousness.

Sometimes, by chance, Haase or Crémieux found themselves near the scuffle. They were careful not to interfere and, on occasion, Haase would even cheer on the aggressors. At the same time, however, you could catch a glimmer of sympathy or a vague uneasiness in their eyes— it was hard to tell which—that reminded you of the mysterious unease which troubles dogs when one of their own is set upon.

Silbermann would get up with his clothes

torn and covered with dirt. I would hurry over to him and pick up his books and papers, which were strewn everywhere. While he was being held, they had pasted all over his face the anti-Semitic labels that were stuck on the wall. His forehead and cheeks would be tattooed with little colored rectangles that read, "Down with the Jews!" I helped him remove them and wiped off his face. His eyes glittered, and he foamed at the mouth. They had pulled his hair, and I neatened it with my hand. They were snickering around us, but I paid no attention. I was conscious of completing my mission, and the idea of glory pushed me far beyond human judgment.

But suddenly, Silbermann, who was never down and out, couldn't refrain from retaliating. Still shaking from his defeat, he would take up the argument again, mockingly defying those around us. You could call it courage, but it was the will to win, urged on by a harsh pride; more than anything else, it was his deep ambition to prove his superiority. And so the fight would rekindle, and again they would rush at him, and I could see him struggling like a piece of worm wriggling under a heel.

Afterwards, I would lecture him and try to explain how clumsy his tactics were. He would answer hoarsely with a fiery look, "How can I help it? The more you oppress us, the more we fight for our rights."

It was true. I noticed now how obsessed he was with revenge. Any occasion seemed right to take an opposing stand, and his superior intelligence served him well; but one time it nearly did him in.

As an assignment, our French teacher had told us to learn any piece of poetry we liked. Thanks to Silbermann, I had just read and was inspired by some verses of André Chénier,* which I then memorized. I asked Silbermann what his choice was, but he kept it a secret. "They'll see . . ." he said with the expression of someone who had a trick up his sleeve.

The recitations began. The less accomplished,

less scrupulous students brushed up on something they had already learned (unbeknownst to the teacher) and were delighted at their lack of effort. The timid ones were thrown by their first taste of freedom; some of them, upon rising, blushed at telling their choice. We all waited with curiosity for Silbermann's turn, aware of his vast knowledge and original taste. The teacher called on him and asked what he had learned.

"Some verses by Victor Hugo, Sir . . . A passage from 'Dieu.'"

He rose and, looking arrogantly around the classroom, began to recite:

> *God! I said God. Why? Who sees Him? Who proves*
> > *He exists?*
> *It's the living that one seeks and the coffin one finds.*
> *Who then can worship? Who then can affirm?*
> *As soon as we think we open a being, we feel it close.*
> *God! maybe a pointless cry, an empty and awful name.*
> *Wish that puts spirit before the inaccessible!*
> *Vain invocation, gone to the edge*

DE LACRETELLE : SILBERMANN

Of the blind precipice where our dreams also go!
Death that carries you, O world, and on which you drift!
Name questioned in deaf dialogues
Between ghost and dream, O night, and between sorrows
And humankind . . .

That first astonishing invocation to God had riveted everyone's attention on Silbermann. Then, as his voice rose, strong and clear, giving every word its power and every thought its weight, we all looked at each other uneasily. We sought reassurance in our neighbors in the face of this apocalyptic vision, this bolt of lightning illuminating chaos, which evoked in each one of us our dreams, our doubts, and our anguish. Gradually, as if they felt strong enough to contend with this audacious annihilator who had risen up amongst them, a rumbling of indignation could be heard. Silbermann's voice drowned out the sound and, barely pausing, he burst forth in a clear, ringing cry:

God! absurd idea or sublime mystery!

There was a tremendous uproar. The teacher intervened and made Silbermann sit down. Once silence was reestablished, he said acidly to Silbermann, "You evidently wanted to show your classmates how tactless you are, M. Silbermann!"

But what did Silbermann care!

I looked at him and could see, despite his outward calm, how triumphant he felt inwardly. He looked over at the group from St. Xavier's, and his nostrils dilated with pride.

The class had calmed down. Montclar furtively passed around a note with directions for a reprise of hostility against Silbermann. Silbermann suspected something, and at the first bell, he ran out the door and across the courtyard. But the others had been quicker, and someone tripped him. He fell very hard, and I saw him writhing on the ground. His face was contorted in pain, but no sound came from his wide-open mouth: the violent shock had interrupted his breathing. I ran over and picked him up and took him to the infirmary at the other end of the school. He let me do so without a word. I held him up, and we walked slowly. At one point he began panting and suddenly stopped short. His complexion, which was generally brown, had turned a frightful purple, and his eyes were unfocused. His lips were trembling, or he was muttering some kind of prayer. A drop of blood ran from a small cut on his forehead.

At the sight of all this, a thought crossed my mind: "What if he were to die! . . ." My imagination, always quick to picture tragic scenes, played out the whole drama, including the events that would ensue. I already could see myself on the following day going up to his executioners, the St. Xavierites, and saying in the most crushing tones, "Well, I hope you're satisfied—you've killed him . . ."

Just then, a reassuring word from Silbermann blew this scenario away, and we continued on our way. He wanted to stop again a little farther on. We were in front of the school chapel, where there was a small square planted with lilacs, and a bench. Silbermann sat down, leaning against the chapel wall underneath a stained-glass window that depicted a group of angels. His hand supported his bent head, and his shadow, echoing the gesture, cast an elongated and curious pattern on the ground.

My mind was so agitated that I began to weave a strange, mystical story around him. I again imagined that he was going to die and I thought that, without a doubt, God would strike him down in order to punish his blasphemies.

He is going to die right here, I said to myself, *on the threshold of this chapel*.

I was deeply troubled and asked myself if Divine Providence hadn't chosen this Catholic church as a place of punishment in order to give me a sign that I should renounce my mission . . .

The sister who received us at the infirmary, in a kind of kitchen full of religious objects, was a shaking, wrinkled, little old woman. Silbermann seemed embarrassed at the idea of speaking to her, so I told her about the violent assault on him.

"Mercy on us!" she said, clasping her hands. "Let him rest a minute. The doctor should be here momentarily, and I'll give him a nice hot cup of tea while we're waiting."

Silbermann was slowly recovering from the shock. His pupils had regained their life and movement. I saw them land like little black demons on the sister's white cap and on the religious statues.

When the sister went into the next room, Silbermann got right up and made me do so, too.

"I feel completely fine, so there's no point in staying. Let's go."

I wanted to wait for the sister's return, but he refused and dragged me outside.

We returned the way we had come. He couldn't stop talking. His pride was back, and he asked me triumphantly if I had noticed La Béchellière's totally scandalized expression during his poetry reading. Then he laughed at the thought of the sister looking all over for us. He turned back toward the infirmary and, crinkling up his features, imitated her quavering voice: "I'll give him a nice hot cup of tea . . ."

I hated this whole performance, and I remembered the words of the Gospel: "A faithless and perverse generation . . ."

"Do shut up," I said impatiently.

This was the first time I had treated him brusquely. He looked at me with surprise and, right away, changing his tone and expression, he put his hand on his chest and said: "I think I'm going to have another choking fit."

One of the teachers had witnessed the violent scene in the courtyard. Because of the dangerous consequences that might have resulted, the aggressor was severely punished, and the incident itself had created enough stir so that nobody dared to openly persecute Silbermann anymore. But his enemies didn't give up the fight; they merely switched tactics. Both of us were quarantined. No one spoke to us during recess or in class. Groups would draw aside in stony silence as we passed by. Now that I didn't have to defend him, I tried to improve his habits as we strolled around the courtyard: this, too, was my mission. I wanted him to get rid of his constant need to fidget, talk, and make himself noticed.

I suggested in a roundabout way that he espouse the principles of inward reserve and discretion that had successfully been preached about in my family. "Don't you take special pleasure," I would say, "in keeping some feelings secret and hiding your thoughts and desires?"

Most of the time he listened to my advice rather mockingly, as if he had sarcastic doubts about these moral standards.

I soon noticed that Silbermann was very sensitive to our state of abandonment. The lack of discussion was an unbearable deprivation for him. He would cast almost melancholy looks at his erstwhile attackers, as if he regretted his harsh feud with them. I was, meanwhile, unhappy with this tranquil state of affairs that no longer demanded any risky service of me. Also, Silbermann's ridiculous habits were magnified in this atmosphere, or, I should say, I noticed them more. Often when I was with him, his physique, his gesticulations, and his voice grated on me so much that I would compare myself to Robinson Crusoe when he was isolated with Friday . . .

Our talks together languished, in truth, because of me. Every year, as vacation drew nearer, with a petty cunning I didn't admit even to myself, I withdrew from my school friends. I didn't want to suffer too cruelly from our separation in the coming months. Toward the middle of June, because of this apprehension, I prudently began to regulate my feelings and affections.

CHAPTER

5

Every summer Aiguesbelles offered the same methodically regulated experience. One could almost say it was as though some superior power had assigned to each of its inhabitants a precise duty they would not flinch from until they died.

My grandfather looked after his property with unvarying care. He would drive out to inspect his vineyard every day before sunset, in every kind of weather, following his own special tracks in the plowed land. One could distinguish his erect figure in the distance silhouetted against the horizon.

My grandmother never stopped moving, despite her age. She was busy all day long on the farm and in the silkworm nursery, her lovely face, with its rosy cheeks, protected by a simple peasant hat. Endlessly preoccupied with improving the property, she decided on changes, effective immediately, that she herself was actively involved in. If, by chance, we came upon her by surprise and found her doing nothing, she became flustered and would rush away, saying, "I must leave you, my children, I have so much to do!"

My mother's duty was to give these two people perfect love. I wonder if her scrupulous conscience didn't reproach her with betraying her parents' love by her love for my father, and if every year she didn't return to Aiguesbelles with the heart of a child seeking forgiveness.

Duty had an exquisite savor in this austere tradition, coupled with great sweetness. I liked assigning myself secret little tasks that I tried to accomplish as well as I possibly could. At dusk, when work on the property stopped, I would go to my room to collect myself.

DE LACRETELLE : SILBERMANN

My room was on the top floor. The walls were whitewashed, and the floor was covered with red tiles. I often looked at a picture hung on the wall. It was a large photograph of one of my uncles, an older brother of my mother's, who was dead and whom I had never known, but whose fierce look and mysterious destiny haunted my thoughts.

My mother had told me much about him. Among her confused childhood memories, she remembered scenes where her brother, at eighteen, obeying some strange vow of renunciation rather than a desire for adventure, had run away from home "to accomplish his mission," as he had written, but what that was, he apparently did not yet know. She told me how, returning after several months, the rebel had remained obstinately silent as to his mysterious vocation, going so far as to curse his parents who tried to keep him home. Finally I learned that at twenty-two he had joined a group of missionaries bound for Madagascar and had died at sea.

I could see most of the estate from my window

and loved watching it as the day drew to a close. I heard the trampling sound of the sheep coming home. On one side, I could see the parallel lines of the vines stretching out into the infinite distance; on the other were the mulberry orchard and the olive grove. As I gazed out at the richness of the land that God had given me to enjoy, I would be filled with a sense of deep gratitude.

"To do good . . . to do good . . ." I would murmur.

"Whom can I save and what can I devote myself to?" I would ask.

I questioned my uncle's picture and was in such an emotional state that I thought I saw in the shadows the lips of the young missionary mouthing an answer.

During the vacation, Silbermann, who had perhaps sensed the cooling off of our relationship and was uneasy about it, did not let me forget him and wrote frequently.

He was motoring across France with his father. His letters described in great detail the places he visited. His critical judgments of people and places were unusual for someone of our age and seemed to me the sign of a superior intelligence. Thanks to his extraordinary memory and thanks, too, undoubtedly, to the ease of a spirit free from all ties, he quickly assimilated everything he saw and created vast panoramas that swamped my narrow vision. These letters were full of historical facts and literary allusions: the one he wrote from Amboise* painted a picture of the court of the Valois* full of blood and gore and poison, thereby justifying my aversion to a dynasty that had brought about the massacre of St. Barthélemy. It also amused him to copy the styles of famous writers. As I have already said, he excelled at this far too well, according to our teacher. While at Chinon he wrote several pages in Rabelaisian* style, which greatly entertained me.

He held forth on monuments and objects of art with a wealth of knowledge gleaned from his father's profession. I was struck by the interest his father showed in religious buildings: I learned that he took long detours to visit small country churches. I attributed this to his artistic tastes—all the more so, because Silbermann wrote enthusiastically about religious architecture.

I myself had always remained unmoved by the beauty of this art. A cathedral, however grand it might be under its sculptured shell, had the same effect on me as some sort of prehistoric monster, unicorn, or dragon that had been preserved throughout the ages. Nothing about it made any sense, and I therefore felt only a vague curiosity with no desire to know more. One of Silbermann's letters on the subject was a revelation for me. Having spent several days in a city famous for the sculptures of its cathedral, he described them to me in their entirety. He showed how the multitude of scenes and ornamentation that seemed like a confused jumble (as far as I was concerned) reproduced all the spiritual and material knowledge of the artisans in the Middle Ages. He made sense out of everything inscribed on those stones. Most important, he gave me a marvelous understanding of the mystical thinking of that period by interpreting one by one the subjects of the religious scenes, commenting on each gesture and relating it to legend. Moving on to the parts relating the life of man, he showed how the bas-reliefs represented the cycle of rural labor: preparing and seeding the land, gathering and harvesting the crops ... The smallest stone was described, down to a garland of leaves, composed entirely, he said, of plants native to the region; he drew the analogy between this humble and primitive decoration and the naïve faith expressed in the religious motifs.

Reading this letter, I remembered hearing Silbermann recite the lines from *Iphigénie* in class. I felt as though a ray of light flooded those monuments that had before seemed so blurred. I remembered the slender ogive arches, the perfect rose windows, the delicate galleries embroidered against the sky, and this art suddenly became worthy of adoration. Gray stone figures I had once gazed at without emotion sprang to my mind newly endowed with a ravishing grace or sadness. I was momentarily confused and blinded by these visions, as by a clear starlit sky after nights of fog.

Upon reading this letter, something Silbermann had once said came to mind: "Can't I understand these things as well as Montclar or Robin? Don't I appreciate them more than they do?"

How could he, who read the traditions of France like an open book, be treated like a stranger? Why should he, who had reached into the essence of our soil, be nearly driven from the country? Those insane attitudes aroused my indignation. I compared them to those that had prepared the way for the revocation of the Edict of Nantes,* which had ultimately lost France— as I had heard many times—her noblest and hardest-working subjects. This analogy greatly strengthened Silbermann's cause in my mind. So, before leaving Aiguesbelles, looking straight into the eyes of my uncle's portrait, I swore never to fail in my mission.

I had hoped that the new school year, with its changes, would help Silbermann's situation. However, the makeup of the class was more or less the same as last year's. On the first day of the term, Philippe Robin walked right by me without a glance. The hatred and hard feelings were still there; our segregation was still there.

Our new teacher was an old man who no longer cared how or what he taught. His chief amusement was to spot his students' weaknesses and watch them act out their trivial dramas. We were simply puppets for him that he maliciously knocked down from time to time. He was immediately drawn to Silbermann's face and gestures and the little tragedy in which he sensed Silbermann to be the lead actor. He saw in him

someone who would entertain him and therefore
made him a star.

Silbermann and I resumed our former inti-
macy. Because of my parents' reactions, I avoided
bringing him home but went to his house almost every day. There I witnessed a scene I remember well.

At the time, new laws regarding forms of wor-
ship and ecclesiastical property were about to
be enforced. On this occasion, the owner of the
Château de la Muette invited the bishops of
France as well as a number of important person-
ages from the Catholic milieu to join him at a
conference to discuss the effects these laws would
have on the clergy. We could see the bishops
accompanied by several serious-looking digni-
taries slowly strolling up and down in the park
and could make out their violet gloves and the
borders of their cassocks. The whole scene was
very grave and resigned and made a strong impression on me. I didn't say a word. Silbermann
stood at the next window; his flashing eyes and

nose flattened against the windowpane gave him a savage look. All of a sudden, grabbing my arm and violently squeezing it, he cried, "Remember this date . . . From this day forward, papal reign is finished in France and will most certainly soon decline in the rest of the world. Remember this date. It may go down in history like those we learn today marking the downfall of governments."

He had left the window and was in a state of frantic agitation. He said other things I didn't understand because his speech had become torrential gibberish, as if he wanted to hasten the destruction he prophesied. Then, turning back to the window and pointing at the assembly of prelates, he said, "The last council."

These words changed his train of thought. And as an odd expression of sensuality crossed his face, he shouted at me, "How Chateaubriand would have described this scene! . . . Do you remember his phrase?"

And after a moment's thought, he declaimed,

"Robbed of their august abodes, the princes of Christendom were assembled in the open air, like the first followers of Christ . . ."

At this moment, any thoughts of literature were far from my mind. I saw defeated adversaries who were so close to me that their ruin affected me as well. I dragged Silbermann away from the window.

Such outbursts were frequent now with Silbermann. His character was changing. He endlessly denounced with bitter irony the injustices and absurdities he perceived; he even went so far as to take a horribly smug pleasure in the misfortunes of others.

But how could one not excuse him, given the profound fear he lived with? I became aware of this one day as we talked quietly when, inadvertently, I gestured with my hand; he must have thought I was going to hit him and quickly covered his face with his arm.

I realized from certain things he said how afraid he was, how he feared his ambitions would be thwarted, and how rejected he felt by us. These feelings frequently drove him to say things like "The French act this way ... The French lack a certain quality ... ," as if he had cut himself off from us.

I did my best to rid him of these ideas and often talked about the impressive social theories he had introduced me to. The seeds he sowed had grown within me, and I dreamt of their coming to fruition.

"It is you," I told him, "with your learning and eloquence, who will make these things happen in France."

But he no longer had the same faith in his ideals and would respond with a skeptical gesture. As to the great role I assigned for him later on, he said with a bitter smile, "You forget that I am a Jew."

"But what's happening now isn't important. This hostility won't last outside the lycée."

"It will last," he continued with flushed cheeks, in a curiously deep voice. "It has lasted for me as long as I can remember. You have no idea what it is like to feel, and to have always felt, that the world is against you. Yes, the whole world. With everyone we meet, even those with no hatred, we sense a mental reservation that wounds us from their looks, and a certain manner. But listen, it's there even in the way one pronounces the word 'Jew' . . . I bet you've never noticed. The lips are pushed forward in a contemptuous pout and then quickly drawn back, as if to avoid contamination while ejecting the word. I have learned to recognize and interpret this movement because I have seen it repeated on the lips of all those who look at me: 'He is Jewish . . . he is Jew-ish.'"

What could I possibly answer? I shuddered when I heard these poignant confidences, as if I had looked into some horrible dungeon and seen a living human being.

At the same time, with a sort of bravado, or perhaps just to cushion his own disgrace, he developed a mania for telling stories in which the people of his race were made objects of derision. He told them brilliantly, imitating a Jewish accent and using vulgar names. Coming from him, these jokes took on a sinister quality. Far from making me laugh, they chilled me to the bone, just as when you hear someone joking about their mortal illness.

My zeal on his behalf redoubled. No other expression can better describe the feeling that drove me on. None of the ordinary feelings associated with that age—ardent friendship, tender thoughts, or jealousy, making it resemble first love—entered into it. On the other hand, the exclusive care, the self-sacrifice, the constant watching over the other person, the unreasonable anxieties, gave this attachment all the attributes of passion. I was constantly tormented by the fear of mishandling my mission and accused myself of imaginary lapses. This nightmarish anguish haunted me at night. I had visions of Silbermann drowning, or lying crumpled at the foot of a cliff; then I would drive into the water or throw myself into space to save him. I would wake up so troubled that, like the friend in the fable,* I would run and wait for him at his front door.

This obvious agitation worried my mother. She questioned me. I answered confusedly, bringing Silbermann's name into my explanations in a way that made her frown. She had heard about my quarrel with Philippe Robin on the subject and severely blamed me for it.

Soon Silbermann's unreasonable demands on my time made me neglect my family obligations and drew a reprimand from my father. I often felt myself watched by him as though some grave accusation hung over me. Although I continued to love both my parents, neither my mother's good counsel nor my father's sound judgment had any influence on my conduct. When, in the evening, having spent the day with Silbermann and followed him, watched over him, and waited on him, I found myself with them again, it was with the detachment of mystic souls in the presence of their earthly loves. Hearing them discuss subjects like my father's promotion or my mother's charities, I felt the same insensitivity mixed with indulgence that mystics feel when they hear worldly chatter. Occasionally my parents would see a vague smile come over my face. This happened when, dreaming about Silbermann's fate, I imagined a sudden reversal of opinion in favor of the Jews, the end of their torment—in short, like the final outcome in *Esther*. More often, however, my imagination liked to paint grim pictures of the future and dire premonitions about everything. This, undoubtedly, was in order to multiply the alluring enticements of devotion and sacrifice.

Thus at the lycée one day, I saw Robin say something to Montclar, who then went over to Silbermann and sneered, "Well, Jew. I hear your father's been caught with his hand in the till."

Silbermann turned ashen but didn't reply.

DE LACRETELLE : SILBERMANN

After this scene, I immediately suspected a plot hatched by Silbermann's enemies and envisioned some incredible disaster befalling him . . .

Alas, this time my foreboding was correct. A few days later, Montclar, Robin, and the other students of St. Xavier, upon arrival at school one morning, produced a newspaper showing that an indictment had been filed against Silbermann's father.

CHAPTER

6

As soon as I could, I went over to Silbermann and asked him a few questions. He answered me as though he were unconcerned, but his hurried tone betrayed his agitation. "What happened to my father is something that happens frequently in his business. He sold as genuine antiques some objects that turned out not to be genuine or that had been restored. He'll take them back and refund the buyer and that will be the end of the story."

He was wrong. The next day, new details said that the sale had been made with false documentation and that the buyer was pursuing the case. This information was supplied by the newspaper

DE LACRETELLE : SILBERMANN

La Tradition Française, which had first published the news and was owned by the Frenchmen for France league. The article added that other more serious charges might be brought against the antique dealer Silbermann.

Two days went by. Silbermann's anxiety grew visibly. When he was with me, he frequently lapsed into deep silences that he came out of with false animation, as people do when they want to deflect suspicion away from themselves.

This stratagem became necessary because the Silbermann affair had become the topic of every conversation at school. Students whispered and pointed at him in the courtyard as he walked by; I could imagine how he was suffering when I remembered what he had confided in me about his sensitivity and always having to be on guard.

La Tradition Française announced one morning that a new complaint had been lodged. This time it concerned the buying and receiving of stolen property. I knew enough about the law to grasp the possible consequences of this. That evening

I rushed out to buy a newspaper and feverishly opened it. I read that the case had been taken up by the public prosecution and that my father had been named the examining magistrate.

It so happened that my parents were out that evening and I was able to cocoon my trouble in solitude, which only blew things out of proportion. I compared my situation to a conflict, abetted by fate, that is the dreadful subject of a tragedy. I lay awake all night hounded by the scenes I foresaw.

As I left for school the next morning, I saw Silbermann waiting for me at the corner.

"Well, do you know what's going on?" he asked right away. "My father is the victim of a terrible plot. I'll tell you all about it. But, first, what did your father say?"

I said that we hadn't discussed anything.

"Listen to me," Silbermann continued. "I want you to know exactly what happened. The Frenchmen for France, either as an act of personal vengeance whose motive we don't know or out of sheer anti-Semitism, have started a campaign against my father. Every day, in *La Tradition Française*, he is insulted at great length and accused of nonexistent crimes. In order to ruin him, they came up with the idea of setting a trap. During our trip to the provinces this summer, my father bought a lot of art objects from churches, which the worthy priests couldn't wait to delete from the state inventory. Obviously, they preferred cold hard cash to their sacred trust as custodians of church property. These purchases were usually made indirectly. And now my father has been accused of buying stolen property on several occasions. He can't confront the sellers, who most probably acted at the instigation of his enemies and have consequently disappeared. Also, having already gotten rid of some things, it's impossible for him to give them back. Those are the facts, and that's what they're basing the case against him on."

He had expressed himself with energy and clarity and was obviously using his considerable skill to persuade me of his point of view. He hardly needed this arsenal, since I was easily convinced. I also remembered what Philippe Robin's uncle had said one day, which confirmed what Silbermann had just told me.

Silbermann took a deep breath and then went on in a deep, moving tone of voice, "That's the truth. It's important that your father know it. I beg you: tell him everything I've just told you. Make him see the facts. Get him to dismiss the case at once for lack of evidence. My father mustn't be indicted. What about my future if he were convicted? What about all those wonderful projects you alone know about: my ambition to write books, to be a great Frenchman? . . . I might even have to leave the lycée . . . What would become of me? Save me from this disaster . . . save me. Remember, you once swore you would do anything in your power for me . . . Now, I can tell you, my fate depends on you."

I interrupted him then. I was choked up with emotion, and I found this emotion so sweet that, out of gratitude, I grasped Silbermann's hands and arms. I promised to speak to my father that night. I was so distraught that I naively believed that my father, on hearing this story, would feel just as I did: I would bring him a magnificent present to share.

That evening, without hesitating but trembling nonetheless, I knocked on the door of my father's study. He called out for me to enter in an even, measured tone of voice.

My father sat working in the narrow room with its dark green upholstery. Behind him in an oak bookcase sat rows of law books, all in the same black cloth binding. His face stood out against this severe background; he had firm features that, while lacking in elegance, radiated an air of nobility, thanks to his extreme stiffness. I said "Good evening" almost inaudibly because as soon as I walked in, my overture suddenly seemed insane. I immediately told him that I had some information for him about the Silbermann affair. I breathlessly poured out everything

DE LACRETELLE : SILBERMANN

I had heard that morning, including the political reasons, the impossibility for my friend's father to prove his good faith, the need for a prompt dismissal of the case in order to stop the attacks: essentially, Silbermann's precise version of what had occurred.

Where did I, usually so overly silent, find the audacity and skill to plead my case? I have no idea. I seemed to have inside my soul some superterrestrial flame that kindled an ardor nothing could extinguish. *My mission*, I kept telling myself, *my mission!*

My father listened to me without interruption. Then he motioned me to draw near.

"Have you seen this man, Silbermann, recently?"

I answered that I had not.

"Then is it your friend who has told you all of this? Was it he, perhaps, who begged you to intervene?"

"It was he who told me the truth, but it's my conscience that brings me here."

"You use words indiscriminately, my child. On the contrary, your conscience should have forbidden you to act in a way that might interfere with the course of justice. I still don't know exactly what your friend's father has been accused of. I do not wish to remember anything you have told me, and I will not let my decision be influenced in any way."

I understood from these words that I had failed in my mission, but with Silbermann's "Save me" ringing in my ears, I felt I must make one last effort to soften my father. I described the torment that cursed Silbermann, his secret agony, and the constant fear he lived in and told him how much all of this touched me. In the hope of arousing his pity, I confided in him stories of my extravagant friendship and my own torment. It was the first time I had analyzed my feelings and, intoxicated by the words, I gave myself away with ingenuous passion. In the heat of the moment, I naively cried out, "I never knew it was possible to have such a feeling for anyone except one's parents!"

DE LACRETELLE : SILBERMANN

With a final gesture I threw out my hands in supplication to my father.

My father stood up. He took my outstretched hands in his. He didn't grip them hard but held them firmly by the wrist, with the feigned gentleness of a doctor. I raised my head toward him, and he looked deep into my eyes.

"This is not a normal feeling to have toward a friend. Where does it come from?"

He had uttered these words with a bluntness that betrayed a hidden meaning. I couldn't answer his question clearly because I would have had to know intimately the most delicate and secret parts of my soul. I made a confused gesture. All of a sudden, as though a sinister gloom were enshrouding me, I caught a glimpse of the base conjecture that had misled him.

I was in such a state of upheaval that after an anguished cry of revolt my sole aim was not to be exonerated but to flee. Ashamed of my father, I turned my face away and tried to wriggle out of his grasp. But now my father squeezed his fingers.

"Confess . . . confess," he said.

I raised my head again. This was no longer my father. His face, which was always stony and rarely showed emotion, had become unrecognizable from the excitement and animation caused by his suspicion and his interrogation. His face was close to mine now, and with glowing pupils and panting breath, he questioned me wordlessly in a cunning, almost complicitous way. I understood as little as an innocent person would the slang of criminals.

Just as suddenly the expression disappeared. My father thought for a moment and then slowly let me go. Raising his index finger, he intoned, "I'll be careful not to condemn you without proof, but listen closely, my son. An overwrought friendship like yours with this boy is always to be avoided. In this particular case, given the current situation between his father and me, it cannot continue to exist. I therefore ask you to no longer consider him one of your friends."

DE LACRETELLE : SILBERMANN

He had regained his usual expression. As I backed out of his study and saw his face full of wisdom and austerity, I realized with a stunned feeling that these irreproachable virtues can lead to inhumane decisions and shameful thoughts.

The next morning, I once again found Silbermann waiting for me on the corner. He anxiously asked me the result of my efforts. I did not divulge what had taken place and said only that my father still had no knowledge of the facts and that he had promised nothing.

"But who would have influence over him?" said Silbermann impatiently. "A colleague? A politician? . . . My father knows several."

I shrugged and disabused him of that idea. Was it reasonable to believe that a man who had so harshly brushed aside his own son's plea would be swayed by a stranger?

Silbermann went on in a dejected tone, "This morning there was another terrible article about my father in *La Tradition Française*. Now that my father's case has been referred to the courts, why can't his enemies spare him?"

Just then we were overtaken by a group of St. Xavier's students on their way to school who, having spotted Silbermann, turned around several times, sniggering and whistling. Silbermann at once straightened up and, taking me by the arm with fake casualness, said harshly, "There! Look at them . . . What cruelty! Yes, I know Christian charity well! But they won't triumph over me. They want to hound me away from here, but I'll fight back. I'll prove to them that I do have the characteristics attributed to my race. After all, I'm not the first Jew to be persecuted."

I felt his fingers digging into my arm.

He may not have been the first, but one might say that this puny little person was burdened by the universal and legendary dislike and disapproval that had been cast at all of Israel. At school, since Silbermann had come to be seen as the son of a crook, those who had teased him for simple fun and not because he was a Jew now changed their attitude toward him. It was as though his disgrace had opened their eyes; they discovered the Semitic traits in Silbermann just as you suddenly notice the protruding ears and deformed thumbs of a man being dragged away by two policemen. With the others, they easily branded him with the convenient cliché "dirty Jew," and without exception they all weighed Silbermann down with the opprobrium of his race. Notwithstanding their political views, they read the royalist newspaper where Silbermann's father was daily described in the most comic and odious light as a thief and looter of churches. Silbermann found copies everywhere, left on his seat in class or slipped into his school bag.

The attacks had resumed and become more and more violent. Silbermann's arrival was watched for, and as soon as he was spotted, the booing began. Then I would rush over and clear a way for him. We would go forward together in the middle of the crowd. I felt inwardly smeared as well by the mocking jokes and insults all around us.

"Thief . . . send him to prison . . ." they'd cry. More than anything, as he had told me, Silbermann feared that the notoriety of his father's affair would oblige him to leave school. So he forced himself to not answer back and make the scenes more violent. Enduring insults and blows with his head lowered, he navigated his way toward the classroom with skillful determination, as if reaching his desk were the only thought in his mind.

As I walked by his side, sharing the same humiliation, I felt a tremendous sense of exaltation: "I have sacrificed everything for him," I said to myself, "the affection of my friends, the good opinion of my parents, and my honor itself." As I thought about these sacrifices, I felt a huge gust of emotion puff up my chest, as if I had suddenly been transported to a high mountaintop.

Even our teachers didn't hide their disapproval of Silbermann. One had relegated him to the last desk in the classroom and barely questioned him in class. Another said nothing about the frequent insults written about Silbermann on the blackboard and even read them out of the corner of his eye. Silbermann noticed these things but never showed it. For the same prudent reasons, he kept his pride and his quick temper under control. I hardly recognized him. Except for a bitter twist of his mouth, as though he had actually swallowed the insults, his expression in these instances remained numb and impassive. One could even say that in order to achieve his goal, he had disguised his young and splendid being under an old cloak inherited from his ancestors, a slavish and shameful garment, but one that could endure.

The disturbances around Silbermann grew to such a point that the headmaster was forced to take steps. He doubled the security in the courtyard and assigned a school employee to stand guard at the entrance of the building and escort Silbermann to class. After that, the rumblings announcing his arrival disappeared, but all the students lined up silently to watch him go by. Silbermann came closer, his face frightfully pale. His eyelids stared down fixedly, but I glimpsed a quick, sharp glance like a dagger piercing its sheath. He stole across the courtyard followed by a man dressed in black wearing a stern, bored expression. This kind of ceremony gave an official sanction to the unfortunate situation, which only aggravated it.

But painful as his position was, Silbermann accepted it.

"Nothing matters," he used to say, "as long as I can stay at school."

Alas! Little did he suspect that the very person in whom he was confiding would be the reason for his departure.

Just as we left school one day, where he must have been painfully insulted—and which might also have been a day when his father was being interrogated—he became very discouraged.

"I'm at the end of my rope," he sighed. "All this hatred surrounding me! . . . I know my dreams will never be realized . . . Why go on like this? . . . I should just leave."

I wanted to comfort him and to have him feel my affection, so I said, "What about me? What would happen to me if you left?"

"You?" he answered quite harshly. "You'd soon forget me and go back to Robin."

"Never," I protested indignantly.

I took his hand and held it in mine. But he continued his lament in a desperate tone that seemed to convey the inevitable outcome so forcefully that I let go of his hand as if surrendering to destiny. I then saw, a few feet away, my mother emerge from the shadows, where she must have been watching me.

"Is this how you obey your father?" she asked in a high, severe tone.

Silbermann, taking off his cap, came toward her and politely held out his hand.

Barely turning toward him, she said coldly,

113

"You ought to understand, Sir, that circumstances have made it impossible for my son to associate with you in any way."

At this insult, an expression of hate instantly came over Silbermann's face that, when superimposed on his first gesture, produced a bizarre, unnatural effect. Stopped short in his bow but still bent over, his body seemed about to pounce; his hand was drawn back and hidden. I sensed in this being, who had been oppressed for so long, such a violent seething that, together with his slightly Asiatic features and curved body, he reminded me of some crazy romantic image, and I thought I would see his hand reappear brandishing a long curved blade over my mother.

He hesitated a moment, gave me a smile that uncovered a clenched jaw, and turned his back on us.

But my mother was already rushing me away. She could not have been more grim had she caught me setting fire to the house. "Wretched child! I suppose you don't think of the consequences of your actions," she said in a shaking voice. "Don't you understand that you risk ruining your father's career? All it takes is for some ill-wisher to publicize your relationship with that boy for your father to be reprimanded, demoted, or even removed from office! And have you given no thought to the fact that you are also jeopardizing your future? This Silbermann, this smooth-talking Jew who leads you around by the nose and sets you against everyone, what does he give you in exchange?... He ruins your friendships; he keeps you away from people who might be useful to you later. You'll have to choose a career soon, map out your course in life ... Who'll give you a helping hand? A shady antique dealer?... Great recommendation! As things now stand, his son and you are like two pariahs at school ... Yes, I know that. I also know that you spend whole days at his house ... How could you have come to this, my child? You, who are so discerning and tactful and so sensitive to our family traditions ... you,

115

who until recently never admired anything that could alienate you from home . . . who used to say proudly when you were little that you wanted to be like your father and grandfather . . . how can you now like those people who come from nowhere and have no sense of values?"

If my mother hoped to win me back by reminding me of these childish vows, she was not successful. On the contrary: already struck by her brutal attack on Silbermann, I felt a growing surprise that drew me away from her as she spoke. That voice I had always heard in praise of goodness and kindness now spoke even more strongly on behalf of self-interest and scheming behavior. How was this possible? I couldn't get over it. When she asked me what advantages I gained from my friendship with Silbermann, I thought for a second in the darkness that had fallen that a woman I did not know had taken her place and was questioning me. I looked at her, stunned. That day she was wearing a simple dark cloak she generally wore when, as secretary of her charity, she was sent to obtain information about a needy family. Her movements stayed hidden under the cloak, and I asked myself if my mother's true thoughts hadn't always been disguised under an assumed austerity.

She did not calm down, and she expected me to either yield or give her a promise. I remained silently obstinate. When we arrived home, as we went our ways, she said, "Since you don't wish to listen to reason, I'll find a way of separating you from this influence."

I didn't see Silbermann the next day because it was a holiday. The day after that, he didn't show up for morning classes. We soon learned that the headmaster had sent a letter to his parents advising them to remove their son from school, given the disruption of which he was the cause.

CHAPTER

7

As I now try to recount my feelings on hearing this news, my memories seem the shards of a dream—and a nightmarish one at that. I find myself back at school, having lost all sense of my surroundings, barely aware of the mocking faces of my companions and indifferent to their sarcasm. Questions buzzed around in my head: "Did my mother get him sent away? What's happened to him? Where can I see him? How can I save him?"

I write him two letters; they remain unanswered. I hang around outside his house in the hopes of meeting him, because now that I know how my name is reviled, I don't dare present myself. Once I bravely question a member of the household as to his whereabouts and am answered vaguely that he has gone out. So I decide to await his return. A garden in front of the house has a gate ajar. I creep in there and, from my watching post in the darkness, I observe the comings and goings in the street. Gripping the iron bars that chill me to the bone, I swear I won't let go until Silbermann appears and I can rush toward him. Every shadow, every passing car, makes me shudder. The hours drift by and night has completely fallen. Finally, with numbed hands and utterly drained, I return home, bitterly reproaching myself for this lack of strength. My parents, having waited a long time, are now finishing dinner. Is this really me, for whom household rules were always sacred, coming home with a haggard face and not a word of excuse? Really me, once so devoted to my mother's serene features, who now allows them to dissolve into anxiety and sorrow? Really me, once so respectful and obedient to my father, who rejects out of hand his demand for an explanation in such a tone of voice that my father, flustered, beats a retreat?

Yes, those scenes were real, but they had the flavor of a dream, or rather, they seemed to take place outside of myself. Everything that night took on such a cloudy aspect that, looking straight into a mirror and catching sight of a fierce face and feverish eyes, I imagined I was back in my room at Aiguesbelles in front of the portrait of my uncle, that strange missionary in revolt against his family.

Ten days elapsed with no word of Silbermann. I had little news of his father's case; I only knew from the newspapers that the preliminary investigation proceeded and that my father had called several witnesses. Finally, I received a letter from him. He suggested a meeting and fixed the date and place, adding, "I leave tomorrow."

The place he settled on was near my house, and I arrived before him. I saw him coming from afar, and it reminded me of our first encounter. He had the same nervous walk and was still frowning and agitated, but this time I knew the enemies were not imaginary.

I ran toward him. Emotion and embarrassment made me stammer incoherently. He interrupted, "I didn't answer your letters because I didn't wish to be the cause of a rift between you and your parents."

His tone of voice was very calm, but I sensed he was holding back. He continued, "Are you aware it was they who asked that I be sent away from school?"

I gestured, deeply distressed.

"Oh, maybe it's all for the best. My situation had become impossible . . . So," he continued a bit shakily, "I leave . . . I leave tomorrow . . . for America."

"You're going to America?" I cried out. "But for how long? When are you coming back?"

"Never," he answered resolutely. "I am going to settle there with one of my uncles."

I was totally dismayed.

"Why make such a decision?" I murmured weakly, taking his hands.

"Why?... Because I have been driven from this country," he said, shaking my hands off.

A passerby noticed his gesture and stood watching us.

"Be careful," Silbermann said sarcastically. "We mustn't stay here. After all, you shouldn't be seen in such bad company."

He led me off to the Bois de Boulogne. We took a narrow path, skirting the fortifications, where no one was in view. I walked silently by his side. My arms, which he had shaken off, hung limply and heavily at my sides.

"Yes," he said, stifling his anger with effort, "I am leaving, I'm giving up my studies and renouncing all my projects. My father's brother, Uncle Joshua, who is a dealer of precious gems in New York, is taking me into his business.

"The Frenchmen for France have won! Think of it. One less Jew among them!... They'll be happy at St. Xavier's when they hear the news! . . . Oh, those idiots! Do they really believe that because they won't see me here, they'll have one less enemy? Don't they realize that because we've always been rejected by everyone, our race has grown in strength over the centuries?"

His voice hissed and the muscles of his neck, taut and swollen, made me think of a nest of serpents standing rigidly erect.

Then, suddenly bursting out, his words shot like sparks from a smoldering fire.

"Why this outbreak of anti-Semitism in France? Why this war against us? Is this a religious war, or the ancient desire for vengeance asserting itself? . . . Nonsense! Your faith is no longer that strong! We mustn't overreach in our search for motives. I'm going to tell you what those motives really are: they are a base egoism and a most contemptible envy. Several years ago, a race of people more subtle, daring, and determined than yours came to your country and succeeded brilliantly in whatever they undertook.

Instead of emulating them in order to achieve the best possible common good, you band together against them and seek to rid yourselves of them. Your hatred is like that in which, sometimes on a team, the person who works the best or the fastest is knifed in the back by the others. This is so true that the classes most implacably fighting us are the middle and upper-middle class because they see growing competition in careers that previously were their private preserve. Just look at the rage with which your friend Robin, who is harmless enough, supports the accusations of his father, the lawyer, and his uncle, the stockbroker. It is this group rather than the aristocracy, which needs our wealth to compensate for its laziness, or the lower classes that altogether ignore this so-called ageless conflict that cry out the loudest, 'Death to the Jews.'

"It's true, there are examples like Montclar, but they are an exception. They occur when the dormant genes of some noble distant ancestor suddenly become aroused and need to find expression in times that are no longer those of the Crusades or of widespread looting. Born violent and hard, contemptuous of reason, and rejecting work or occupation, these people fling themselves unthinkingly into any kind of feud, however disastrous and treacherous it might be; ultimately, they become anachronisms in our society and go and get themselves killed in Africa.

"How do you justify your aversion to a Jew? By the horrible characteristics traditionally attributed to him? . . . They are all absurd. His stinginess, for example? . . . Look around you at these houses . . ."

He pointed out the wealthy neighborhood, recently established in La Muette, near the Bois de Boulogne. All these buildings conveyed a sense of luxury and extravagance.

"There is the house Henri de Rothsdorf is building for his collections. Behind it is Raphaël Léon's, who copied a Louis XVI lodge. This tall roof belongs to Gustave Nathan and is said to be the finest building in Paris. Next to it is the one I live in, and that of the Sachers and the Blumenfelds. I could tell you the name of every person in this area, and they're all Jewish. But it's not bad, is it? We do things in style! ... What else? Jews are dirty? ... Really? Do you think you'll find more bathrooms in these houses or in those of the Faubourg St. Germain?* ... Are they predatory, too? ... Doesn't everyone who works want to make money? ... Are they robbers? ... My friend, if you knew the sordid deals that the finest names in France come to my father with, you would agree that our way of getting rich is entirely honest. If you had heard, as I did one day, the scene that took place at our house between my father and the Duke of Norrois, you would see the light. Norrois had robbed my father in some deal, literally robbed him, and my father had found out. I could hear him yelling next door, 'What? You did that?' with no 'Your Grace' about it! ... And then I heard the duke begging, 'Calm, my dear Silbermann, you must be calm . . . I'll repay everything . . . I give you my word of honor, you'll be compensated.' The next day, the Duchess of Norrois sent my mother flowers, but my father was never reimbursed for what he had lost. He never filed suit.

"I know, I know . . . it's not just our personal characteristics you object to. There is also the more serious question of governance: We are a State within the State; our race is not assimilated and never adapts to the general character of a country . . . What do you think? How could it be possible otherwise? For centuries we have lived penned up like cattle with no possible connection to the outside world. In certain countries, not even a hundred years ago, our houses were chained off. Do you expect those hereditary bonds to be untied from one day to the next? And can't you see that your policy of hatred only reaffirms them? And isn't every one of us, in spite of being citizens of the same nation, subjected to the influences we have inherited, like class and religion? I may be a Jew, but aren't you every bit a Protestant with your scrupulous conscience, your solemn pacts, your underhanded proselytizing, and your sentimentalizing, all of which you disguise under a mask of reserve? You most certainly have remained true to your Calvinist ancestors. Between a Montclar, descendant of a caste of chiefs who rebel against even their prince; a La Béchellière, the son of mediocre country squires who can't see beyond the boundaries of their land; a Robin, whose family has only gained status since the Revolution; and you, of humble Huguenot extraction . . . you are all as completely different as there are distinct types of races and create just as many elements of conflict."

I tried to say something, but he cut me off with an imperious gesture and heatedly began again.

"But that isn't all. Your great grievance is against the Jewish spirit, that famous Jewish spirit whose dangerous instinct for gratification corrupts every kind of nature and prevents the creation of anything lasting and debases thought ... Don't you think a bit of this practicality would benefit you? Wouldn't men who could teach you how to use to better advantage your time on earth bring to this country, divided between past and future visionaries, just what it needs? And if this new sensuous blood, mingled with yours, were to increase your capacity to feel, you would not become animals, as certain people fear. The brilliant intelligence of Israel has shone enough through the ages for you to be reassured on this point."

He collected himself for a moment. His passion seemed spent, and he went on in a voice full of strange poetry.

"To be both Jewish and French—what a fruitful combination that might be! I had such hopes for it! I didn't want to overlook anything you had written or thought. You can't imagine my feelings when I discovered some beautiful work born of your genius! You've seen me at those times. I would become silent, and you could question me in vain because I felt that beauty becoming a part of me, my worthless Jewish soul.

"I remember the day I first read *Mémoires d'Outretombe*.* I was only familiar with the *Génie du Christianisme* and had misjudged Chateaubriand. I didn't like his cold, pompous descriptions. Then suddenly I see Combourg before me; I discover the passage on America, on emigration, and I am swept into the prodigious currents of this brain ... An amazing fever took hold of me! I devoured the eight volumes in less than a week. I read through part of the night, and when I had put out the light and closed my eyes, certain sentences lingered on in my head like fireworks that kept me awake.

"I remember, too, the hours spent in going over, again and again, my plans for the future: first, what kind of education would I pursue after school and what would I do after graduation? I didn't feel impatient because I didn't want to be guilty of the haste and overeagerness that people like me are accused of. Nonetheless, I dreamt of the day I would see my name in print. Well, that wish has come true. My name has been in print and even followed with a description in *La Tradition Française*: 'Silbermann junior, a hideous Jewish abortion . . .' And so you have beaten me down, I who only thought of how I would serve you."

His voice choked. He stopped and lowered his head, with tears streaming down his cheeks.

This bizarre tirade, this mixture of laments and curses, had moved me to both pity and disaffection. I took advantage of his distress to answer him.

"But I haven't acted that way," I protested. "I gave you everything and would have sacrificed anything and have proved it many times over!"

Then, lifting his head and brusquely changing his tone: "Don't you think I deserved it? With all due respect to your mother, that worthy Protestant, who practiced her evangelical charity on me so well, you can be sure that my friendship was more valuable to you than any other. Remember our talks and everything I taught you and made you understand? Did you get any such advantages from your other friends or even your family?... Go on, answer me ... I only have to recall the expression on your face as you listened to me and to repeat your own words. One time you told me that during our conversations, you felt that more ideas came to you more quickly, and that you could develop them more intelligently ... Well, it would seem worth a great deal to be able to exert such an influence over another person. The ability to stimulate someone else's intelligence is not, as far as I know, granted to inferior human beings ... That is the overwhelming fact: we are more gifted than others. We are superior. If you aren't convinced, count our numbers throughout the world: seven million ... eighty thousand in France ... then look at our place in that world. Remember what I'm going to say: the chosen race is not some crazy prophet's rambling on, but an ethnological truth you must accept."

He stopped and wet his lips, which looked swollen after this passionate outburst. As he spoke, he had walked onto a small elevation in front of me from which he dominated the surrounding space. An expression of pride lit up his face through his tears: Zion had risen from its ruins.

The azure sky that day was stunning. On one side the sun, nearing the horizon, shone with an orange light that conjured up hot southern climes, while opposite and higher, the pale, cool moon, partially hiding under a snowy cloud, transported one north. Against this background, which seemed to encompass the universe, Silbermann's silhouette stood out like an allegorical vision. The air trembled with his words and was whipped up by his arms. He seemed lord of the world.

"Do you understand how I've been wronged?"

he went on. "And can you still ask me why I'm leaving France with no intention of returning?... Oh, I know! I could have lived through these difficult beginnings through habit or patience, like so many others of my race, but I'm leaving them to you. You see, every country has the Jews it deserves ... those are Metternich's words, not mine.

"Now I've woken up from my dreams. I'm going to make money in America. With my name, I was predestined to, right?... David Silbermann looks better on a diamond merchant's business card than on a book cover! I wasn't prepared to embark on this profession, but my future doesn't worry me; I'll know how to pull through. Over there, in the tradition of my forefathers, I'll get married. What nationality will my children be? I don't know and I don't care. Those countries hardly count for us. Wherever we may be throughout the world, isn't that place always a foreign land? One thing I do know for sure: they'll be Jewish and I'll make good Jews out of them. I'll show them the greatness of our race and respect for our beliefs. Then, even if they're ugly like me, have a tormented soul like mine, and suffer as much as I have, it won't matter because they'll know how to survive and overcome their ordeals. They will be sustained by those invincible secrets we hand down from generation to generation and by that tenacious hope that for centuries has made us solemnly intone, 'Next year in Jerusalem.' No, I'm not worried about what they will become. If the power of money becomes their motivating force, they'll follow in the steps of their ancestors. And if this almighty principle is shaken and a new one appears to upset the old order, then they'll change their name and profession. They'll adapt to the ruling ideas, while you poor fools will either oppose them or submit to them, but you won't profit by them.

"There. I'm finished. I wanted someone to hear all these things. Now we have nothing left to say to one another. Good-bye."

He touched my shoulder in a final gesture, leapt down the slope in three bounds, and in a final moment disappeared, like a prophet who becomes invisible to those he has come to warn.

I let him go without a word or gesture. I felt stupefied. After a few minutes, while the words I had just heard echoed within me, I looked around the deserted ramparts. Far away, at the foot of a bastion, a group of soldiers was practicing bugle calls. They looked like miniature toys.

CHAPTER

8

That was my last talk with Silbermann. Although the strangeness of our parting made the separation less painful, I was profoundly sad once he was definitely no longer a part of my life. The reason was not that I no longer saw him or even that our friendship ended, but that I missed the enthusiasm my glorious mission had inspired within me each morning. I couldn't resign myself to a daily routine without noble goals after having become accustomed to hard effort and necessary sacrifices. Love had lost all meaning and seemed horribly purposeless.

Silbermann, while introducing me to all kinds of new ideas, had destroyed most of those

I possessed. And now that his quick and lively intelligence was no longer there to seduce me, I became aware of how little remained.

This was true of every aspect of my life.

Always inclined to contradict and criticize, Silbermann had made me see the flaws in things. In literature, he would back up his praise of one thing by tearing down another, and since his taste often changed, he would subtly belittle a work that a short while before he had rated above any other. I had listened too well. With his constant criticisms, he had succeeded in showing me the imperfections of everything I'd read, and now when I reread a book I had previously loved, I no longer felt the same unbridled enthusiasm. The misleading idea that all qualities are relative poisoned my pleasure in reading and dampened my curiosity. Finally, thanks to Silbermann's confused and superficial teaching, I saw in everything people have written only a barren recycling of ideas and images throughout the centuries. As I stood in front of my bookcase, it was as though I had inherited from the young Jew's greedy intelligence the well-known satedness of one of his Hebrew kings, and I recalled the passage from Ecclesiastes: "For what advantage hath a man for all his labor? All is vanity and vexation of spirit."

But it was at home that the destruction Silbermann had caused within me was most apparent. There, all my gods had toppled and all my illusions about honor, beauty, and the customs and beliefs of my family were gone. And my parents' authority would soon suffer the same fate.

For some time, I had worshiped them blindly. On a couple of occasions I had suspected that some of their values had always escaped me. I hadn't forgotten my father's weird expression when he had so passionately accused me of disgraceful conduct, or my mother's less-than-noble arguments when she tried to break up my friendship with Silbermann.

One evening they were in the drawing room, and I was just about to go in when I heard Silbermann's name mentioned. I stopped in the doorway, hidden by a curtain.

"His guilt is unquestionable," my father was saying. "But one can say, after all, that the charges against him are not very precise."

"If that is so, my dear, consider how useful the support of an influential deputy would be. If you do what Magnot is asking, he will be eternally grateful."

I raised the curtain and went in.

My mother stopped talking. She and my father immediately assumed the serious and quiet expression that they always wore when we sat down to dinner. Under the light of the chandelier, the everyday scene and the usual ritual were being played out for me. The quick change in their expressions, however, hadn't prevented me from catching a look of greed mingled with insistence on my mother's face and a kind of vacillation on my father's. I suddenly remembered a question Silbermann had asked me one day: 'Who could influence your father?... a politician?. . . My father knows several.' I saw that certain strings had been pulled on behalf of Silbermann's father, and that my mother, hearing about this, was hardheadedly evaluating the situation to see what benefits could be drawn from it, and that my father, the magistrate—who had always set a standard of the highest integrity for me—was hesitating and even leaning toward committing fraud.

I sat down between them. My thoughts were uncertain. I felt as if the ground on which I had so far firmly stood were suddenly crumbling. I don't know if my parents suspected that I had overheard their conversation, but I do remember a certain embarrassment on their part as they watched me out of the corner of their eyes. The meal began in silence.

I recalled the sermon on the integrity of justice my father had preached to me in his study and his majestic, almost god-like emphasis on the word *conscience*. And I recalled the severe blame my mother often cast on other people's actions. "They don't act as they would like me to believe," I said to myself. "They deceive me, and they have always deceived me."

This idea threw a new light on my past. I had often compared my parents' conduct and their system of values to the tapestries my mother would embroider patiently every evening. Now I seemed to discover for the first time the reverse side of her work; behind the symmetrical lines and beautiful, finely toned ornamentation lay a tangle of threads, knots, and loose ends.

My parents made a few pleasant remarks to me, to which I replied in monosyllables. Staring blankly ahead, I seemed to see again, as if the tapestry had unfolded before me, their simple gestures, strict beliefs, and noble actions, and each one of these beautiful images was woven around some horrible woof. What did I care, now that what they were plotting would save Silbermann's father! With the sudden upheaval of my moral values, I forgot about all that.

The following day, I prayed with all my heart

and soul that my father wouldn't succumb to the pressure being exerted on him and hoped that the proof would lie in the arraignment of the antique dealer. "His guilt is unquestionable," my father had affirmed, and I trembled at the thought that he should pronounce a judgment contrary to this conviction.

Several days later, my mother drew me aside with a mysterious and conspiratorial look and told me that since I was interested in the father of my old friend, I could be reassured about his fate: the result of the inquiry was favorable and would undoubtedly be endorsed by the prosecutor's office. And so my father's conscience, hardened against any appeal for pity, had yielded to the motive of personal gain.

I listened to my mother with such a look of contempt that she blushed and turned away.

Shortly afterwards, an order of insufficient cause was handed down in favor of Silbermann's father. By an irony of fate, what we had both so passionately hoped for probably barely affected

Silbermann in his new country, and I heard it with tears of shame. It only confirmed my father's baseness.

Because of this result, I boiled with a feeling of rebellion toward my parents. I was furious they had not practiced the rigid moral principles they had indoctrinated in me, and I thought of the difficult and narrow path I had always strived to follow. Toward what goal? Of what use was this painful subjection to rules? Sometimes in the street, out of a desire to impose a small duty on myself, I walked along the line at the sidewalk's edge. Wasn't that the same way I lived my life, barely looking at things and obsessed by rules that were just as rigorous and absurd?

I counted up all the deprivations I had inflicted on myself and all the constraints I had submitted myself to when I held back my overly fiery emotions and repressed my natural desires with the same care and joy my grandfather felt in pruning his vines.

DE LACRETELLE : SILBERMANN

I felt that my childhood trust had been abused and I rose up, secretly violent, against the people who had duped me. I avoided my parents as much as possible and gradually even stopped speaking to them. I have no idea what they thought of my behavior because I pretended to ignore their presence and didn't even look at them. Sometimes I would glance at them in a mirror or a polished surface and would see my mother's despairing look fixed on me.

Time passed. I lived in a state of utter disillusionment, with no faith in virtue and no taste for evil.

One evening when I returned home, I saw my mother, who had come to meet me in the hall. She had a newspaper in her hand and said with great joy, "Your father has been made a judge. The news will be officially announced this evening."

When I heard this, in spite of my effort to remain unmoved, I couldn't repress my interest.

DE LACRETELLE : SILBERMANN

My family had waited years for this promotion. The subject had been discussed again and again; I knew it was an important step in my father's career, and the great effort my mother had made to hurry it along. "A seat on the bench," she had so often exclaimed, clasping her hands. In spite of myself, all of these thoughts churned in my mind.

My mother undoubtedly sensed my turmoil. Gravely, she spoke these simple words: "My child, will you not join us on this happy day?"

I raised my eyes to her face, which I had stubbornly avoided doing for a long time. As if finding her face again made me see it better, I discovered certain signs I'd never noticed before: a weariness in her eyes and a thinning of her hair around the temples. I saw for the first time that her face was not formed, as children believe of their parents, of unchangeable perfect flesh but that it was, on the contrary, perishable and already worn. I don't know what feelings my eyes may have betrayed, but I saw my mother lower her head and make a gesture of despair. Then, bursting into tears, I threw myself into her arms.

I wept tears not only of tenderness or remorse; I cried because of the misery weighing upon me. I had realized when I saw the fragility of that pure face that no soul, however virtuous and saintly, can rise above human imperfection. I had understood that an impossibly high moral standard is unattainable for any of us. And I thought sadly that I would have to give up the unrealistic goals I had set for myself.

I'm sure my mother knew the real reason for my tears because she suddenly looked sad and humiliated. She might have confided in me then, confessing how much she had suffered and telling me about her moral struggles and weaknesses. I wanted, however, to spare her any confession and laid my forehead gently against her trembling lips.

Lightly dragging me, she pushed open the door of my father's study. My father smiled and left his work to come toward us. He kissed me on the forehead. The three of us stood together for a moment until the maid came in to say dinner was ready. Then my father playfully recited from the parable of the Prodigal Son: "Let us eat and make merry, for this my son was dead and is alive again; he was lost and is found."

My mother, with a wonderful gesture, pretended to wrap me in a beautiful cloak and to put a ring on my finger.

After Silbermann's departure from the lycée, I fell back into the isolation to which my friendship with him had condemned me. Obstinately morose, I remained as sullen and withdrawn at school as at home. After all, could any of them replace Silbermann? Which of them, even among those who appreciated the things of the mind, had the intellectual passion of the young Israelite? Everyone else seemed weak and vapid when I compared them to Silbermann and remembered his endless curiosity and his ability to make abstract ideas intoxicating and alive.

DE LACRETELLE : SILBERMANN

Nevertheless, I could easily have resumed some friendships because the reason for my ostracism was gradually forgotten. Outside of school, political activity had died down and the Frenchmen for France league had lost much of its importance. At school, anti-Semitic sentiments had ceased for several reasons. For one thing, there were more Jews every day and they were, therefore, less conspicuous. Also, Montclar had been expelled for some serious wrongdoing involving a teacher, and without their leader, his companions were calmer. La Béchellière went back to his cold, supercilious manner, and Robin had resumed his harmless pleasures.

I scarcely gave Robin a thought and didn't try to get in touch with him.

One spring day I saw him in class looking dreamily out the window with uncharacteristic seriousness. One could see through the glass panes the first green buds against a blue sky. His gaze suddenly turned and fell slowly on me and then turned away again when I didn't respond.

149

DE LACRETELLE : SILBERMANN

After my initial surprise, I was deeply moved by this tentative attempt at reconciliation. Without really knowing why, I thought of the dove flying away after the dark days of the flood, and I felt that a clear sense of peace about everything would come soon. But whether out of pride or weakness neither of us made a move, and several weeks went by with no further developments.

Spring that year was prematurely warm with little rain, and the atmosphere under the burning sky was stifling.

In my loneliness, I was particularly sensitive to the drought. My whole being felt weak, and I dreamt of a new source that would refresh my life.

On the way home one evening, I went by St. Xavier's at the end of the school day. It was warm, and the sun was setting behind some clouds. Suddenly, with no warning clap of thunder, big raindrops began to fall in the still, quiet air. I sought shelter under a scaffolding just as some students came scurrying across the road.

DE LACRETELLE : SILBERMANN

The younger ones, who still wore the school uniform—a short blue jacket and a cap with a velvet band—began to run and shouted with joy at the sky, spreading their arms under the long-wished-for, much-needed rain.

I watched them from my little corner and shrugged my shoulders. Because of either my reserved nature or my rather puritanical upbringing, I had always considered free, unrestrained expressions of joy as offensive and foolish. But there was something so nice and frank and open in the movements and expressions of these boys who seemed so much happier than I was that I wanted to join them and share in the same delightful baptism . . .

Just then, someone with his head down to protect himself against the rain came to seek shelter beside me. When he raised his head, I recognized Philippe Robin. He blushed and looked embarrassed when he saw me, but he smiled faintly. Without saying anything, I drew a little aside to give him room, and as I did so, I saw a picture behind us on the wall. It was a charcoal caricature representing a coarse likeness of Silbermann. The features were faded, but they had been notched into the stone and were recognizable: the hooked nose and pendulous lips overhanging the thin neck. The words underneath were still legible: "Death to the Jews."

Robin's glance had fallen on the wall at the same time. He blushed even more, hesitated a second, and then murmured in a humble, almost tender voice, "Shall we forget about all that and become friends again?"

Forget?... Was that possible? The sight of that sketch and the words below it had rekindled an intense, almost mystical feeling within me. I thought of what I had called my mission, my initial promise and long struggle, all my efforts to save Silbermann; I remembered the extraordinary shudder that went through me when, standing beside him, scorned and beaten like him, I repeated to myself, "I am sacrificing everything for him." No, these things could

152

never be forgotten. The slightest word of reconciliation would be a betrayal. I had the feeling I couldn't speak and I remained savagely silent, standing stiffly with my teeth clenched.

As I went over these trials in my mind, I realized that the path on which I was engaged was difficult, steep, and with a thousand obstacles; one must climb it without resting, and the slightest stumble means a fall. I envisioned a painful and arduous life of being torn apart day by day. And to what end? Didn't I now know that no one could survive at the heights to which I once had aspired?

Philippe Robin was waiting for my answer and didn't say anything, but he watched me out of the corner of his eye. His face was happy and calm. He seemed to have taken a much easier, more comfortable, and safer path—a path that skirted the abysses but was never lost in them.

I felt as though I were at the crossroads of these two paths and my future happiness depended on my choice between them. I hesitated

DE LACRETELLE : SILBERMANN

... Suddenly the landscape on Philippe's side seemed so appealing that my whole being relaxed. I smiled a little, and Philippe, sensing my acquiescence, put his hand on my shoulder. The rain had stopped. He led me away.

As I started off with him, I looked back at Silbermann's caricature and, with an effort, said in a slightly mocking tone, so perfectly natural it surprised me, "It's a very good likeness."

NOTES

Page 19, *Iphigénie*. A play by Jean Racine (1639–1699) that is considered one of the classics of French literature. As with many of his plays, Racine turned to classical literature for inspiration—in this case, Euripides' *Iphigenie*.

Page 22, Ranelagh Park. A park in Paris's sixteenth *arrondissement* (district), with majestic trees, wonderful promenades, and playgrounds for children.

Page 23, Pierre de Ronsard (1524–1585). French poet and leader of the literary group "La Pléiade" (see page 56). Ronsard was a poet at the court of Charles IX and was hostile to the Reformation. His work fell into oblivion until the nineteenth century, when it was rediscovered by the famous French critic Sainte-Beuve.

NOTES

Page 24, Jean de La Fontaine (1621–1695). One of the great French poets, La Fontaine is particularly known for his "fables," which often have moral endings.

Page 25, Alphonse de Lamartine (1790–1869). French poet and politician. His first lyrical work, *Méditations poétiques* (1820), catapulted him onto the literary scene and inspired the new generation of romantic poets, who adopted him as their master. Lamartine also used his writing talents to promote liberalism in politics (*Histoire des Girondins*, 1847). He was a member of the provisional government in 1848 and became the minister of foreign affairs. But after losing the presidential elections by a large margin in December 1848, he withdrew from politics and dedicated most of his time to penning autobiographical works.

Page 26, Hyppolite Taine (1828–1893). French philosopher, critic, and historian. Throughout his work, Taine developed a deterministic vision of man. He conceived of art and literature as natural human functions whose manifestation in the artist

NOTES

depended on three factors: race, time, and the environment. In his *Philosophie de l'art* (1882), Taine melded his esthetics to his determinism and defined art as the witness of the spiritual evolution of societies.

Page 31, Frenchmen for France. The subtitle of an anti-Semitic newspaper, *La Libre Parole* (Free Speech), launched in 1892 by writer, pamphleteer, and journalist Edouard Drumont. The subtitle, *La France aux français* (France for Frenchmen), was an obvious reference to the paper's xenophobic and anti-Semitic bent. Drumont used *La Libre Parole* to take a violent stand against Alfred Dreyfus during the Dreyfus affair. He was also the author of *La France Juive*, a virulently anti-Semitic book and national best-seller.

Page 39, *Les Misérables*. An epic novel by Victor Hugo, published in 1862, that traces the ascension of the hero Jean Valjean from wretchedness to nobility, creating the social fresco of nineteenth-century literature.

Page 39, *Oeuvres de Paul-Louis Courier*. A volume con-

NOTES

taining the works of the French political pamphleteer Paul-Louis Courier (1772–1825). Courier wrote several pamphlets against the government of the Restoration in France and was subsequently arrested and condemned to several months of prison in 1821. Four years later, during a stroll in a forest around his property, he was murdered.

Page 43, *Esther*. Jean Racine's tragedy (1689) based on the book of Esther in the Old Testament.

Page 47, Alfred de Vigny (1797–1863). French writer and author of lyrical poems (*Poèmes antiques et modernes,* 1826). Vigny illustrated the romantic conception of theater in *Chatterton* (1835) and expressed throughout his work the tragic destiny of genius condemned to solitude and the general indifference of nature and humankind alike. His position was that against this state of affairs, the man of genius can show only stoic resignation.

Page 47, François-René de Chateaubriand (1768–1848). French writer elected to the Académie Française. Chateaubriand traveled extensively and worked as an ambassador. His masterpiece, *Mémoires*

NOTES

d'Outretombe (see page 130), is an autobiographical account of his life and times.

Page 56, The Pleiades ("La Pléiade"). A group of seven French poets from the latter half of the sixteenth century that included Pierre Ronsard, Jean du Bellay, Jean-Antoine de Baïf, Pontus de Tyard, Étienne Jodelle, Rémy Belleau, and Jacques Peletier du Mans. Together, they proposed to restore inspiration and form to French poetry.

Page 56, Jules Michelet (1798–1874). French historian and author of the monumental *Histoire de France* (1833–1846) as well as the *Histoire de la Revolution française* (1847–1853). Through his teaching at the prestigious Collège de France, he promoted liberal and anticlerical ideas.

Page 57, "Conversation of the Marshal d'Hocquincourt" (in full, "La Conversation du Maréchal d'Hocquincourt avec le Père Canay"). This radical and witty piece on religion, written in 1665, was composed as a dialogue between a soldier and a Jesuit priest. The author, Charles de Saint-Évremond (1613–1703), was known as a skeptic and a libertine

NOTES

because of his radical ideas, and he fled France after falling out of favor with Louis XIV.

Page 59, Amiel's *Journal intime*. Henri Frédéric Amiel (1821–1881) was a Swiss writer from Geneva and a true romantic. In his *Journal intime*, or "intimate diary," published posthumously in 1883, he scrutinizes his soul and blames his extreme sensitivity and timidity for his lack of action. Paralyzed by life, he was prone to constant bouts of anxiety and melancholy.

Page 59, André Chénier (1762–1794).
An eighteenth-century French poet actively involved in the French Revolution. Appalled by the excesses of the revolutionary period known as "the Terror," Chénier openly protested against the regime and was executed. His work *Les Iambes* is a masterpiece of political satire.

Page 83, Amboise. A small city in France known both for its castle built as an artistic center by Charles VIII in 1492 and for its fifteenth-century manor, Clos Luce, where Leonardo da Vinci lived for a few years and eventually died.

NOTES

Page 83, Court of the Valois. The Valois was a dynasty of kings that reigned over France between 1328 and 1589. On August 24, 1572, Charles IX, one of the Valois kings, ordered the mass murder of Protestants. The massacre, started at dawn on that day, is known today as the "massacre de la Saint-Barthélemy."

Page 83, Rabelaisian. The Rabelaisian style refers to the style of French Renaissance writer François Rabelais (1494–1553), who is known for his licentious verve, mixing erudite and scatological vocabulary, along with invented words.

Page 86, Edict of Nantes. On April 13, 1598, in the city of Nantes, King Henry IV regulated the legal status of the reformed church in France in an edict. The Protestants were given the right to practice their religion and were considered an official body with legal rights. The Edict of Nantes was revoked in 1685 by Louis XIV.

Page 94, "like the friend in the fable." The fable referred to here is "Les deux amis" by Jean de La Fontaine.

NOTES

Page 126, Faubourg St. Germain. An aristocratic neighborhood in what is now the seventh *arrondissement* (district) of Paris. The area came into being at the beginning of the seventeenth century, when Marguerite de Valois, known as Queen Margot, decided to take up residence on the left bank of the River Seine and had a palace built for herself. Over the course of the eighteenth century, the Faubourg St. Germain became the "anti-Versailles," where aristocratic families lived away from the bustle of the court.

Page 130, *Mémoires d'Outretombe*. A multivolume memoir by François-René de Chateaubriand that spans his entire life and times and is considered to be his masterpiece.

Discussion Questions

1. What hints does the novel offer about the social and political climate in France during the early 20th century? Give specific examples.

2. What risks did the narrator take to maintain his close friendship with Silbermann? Are most people willing to take such risks? Why or why not?

3. In what ways does the age of the two main characters affect the story? How might the story have been different if Silbermann and the narrator were middle-aged adults?

4. How would you describe the narrator's views of himself and his friend Silbermann?

5. How did Silbermann's persecution affect his personality? What character traits—both

positive and negative—did his persecution bring forth?

6. What would this story have us understand about the traditions and values of Protestantism? What was the situation of Protestants in France at the time of this story?

7. What are we to think about the verdict that was reached in the case of Silbermann's father? Was it surprising? What were the repercussions of that verdict?

8. Who and/or what did Silbermann betray in the end? Who and/or what did the narrator betray?

9. Was the narrator's change of heart regarding his parents and his friend predictable or surprising? If he had *not* had a change of heart, how might the book have ended?

10. What does the novel say about the notions of honesty, sincerity, and being true to oneself?

PRODUCED BY WILSTED & TAYLOR
PUBLISHING SERVICES

Production management: Christine Taylor
Copyediting: Melody Lacina
Design: Jeff Clark
Composition: Melissa Ehn

Printed in Canada by Transcontinental Printing